All That's Unspoken

Sunnydale Days, Book One

Hearts, horses and healing

Constance Phillips

ALL THAT'S UNSPOKEN
Copyright © 2015, Constance Phillips
Trade Paperback ISBN-10: 1944363017
ISBN-13: 978-1-944363-01-7

Editor, S.R. Paulsen
Cover Art Design by Calliope-Designs.com

Digital Release, December 2013
Trade Paperback Release, May 2015

Media > Books > Fiction > Romance Novels
Category/Tags: romance, contemporary, Small town, Friends-to-lovers, sweet romance, holiday romance, second chance at love, therapeutic horse riding

DEDICATION

This book is dedicated to the people in my life who can easily read the things that are unspoken between us: my husband and children.

ALL THAT'S UNSPOKEN

Hailey Lambert came home for the holidays to help her father. Instead, eight years later, she is forced to face all that was left unspoken between her and high school crush, Nate.

After eight years, Hailey is back in Caseville Michigan. Just months after her mother's death, her siblings want to put their father in a nursing home and rent out the family farm. If that wasn't enough, the prospective tenant is Nate, the high school crush she left behind the day after they acted on their mutual attraction.

After high school, Nate Jenkins planned to leave small town behind, but life dealt him a different hand of cards to play. He's now back in Caseville, raising his daughter, and running his family's diner. His daughter's speech disorder has been improved by therapeutic horse riding and if he can lease the old Lambert farm, he can get her a horse of her own. The only standing in the way is Hailey, the same woman who left him eight years ago without even saying goodbye.

Can they get over all that's unspoken between them?

Chapter One

The squeak of the barn door rolling down the metal rail cut through the silence of the night air. It wasn't as heavy as Hailey remembered, but then again her fondest memories of the barn were from when she was a lot younger.

Her cousin Rhonda laughed as she walked past her then went straight to the light switches, flipping them on. "Quiet or we're going to get caught."

"I think we're old enough to be in the barn after dark." Hailey pushed the door closed to block the biting wind. Still, it slammed against the walls, causing the aging building to moan and creak in protest, mimicking the mood of her heart as she remembered the events of the last year.

"Think fast!" Rhonda pulled a beer can from the pocket of her coat and then tossed it in Hailey's direction. "Uncle Bill isn't going to ground us for sneaking beer?"

Hailey looked at the label a moment before cracking it open. A rush of memories accompanied the sound and scent. "What were we? Sixteen?"

"I think so. Wasn't that the summer after my family moved to Saginaw? Your mom and dad let me come and stay with you for a couple of weeks."

"Thanks for coming out here with me. I needed a

break from all the holiday cheer,"

Rhonda hoisted herself up on the gate separating the barn aisle from the open arena, straddling it as if it was a horse.

Hailey leaned against one of the stall doors, and raised the can toward her cousin. "Merry Christmas." She then took a long sip before continuing. "Jake and Kelly think Dad needs to be put in a nursing home, you know. They've been trying to nail me down to 'talk about it' since I got home yesterday morning."

Rhonda exhaled and slid back on the top of the gate until she was leaning against the wall. "I thought he was fine at dinner, a little tired maybe, but aren't we all? My mom says he has moments, though."

"That's what they say too. I haven't seen any signs."

"On the drive up here Mom was saying she feels like she owes it to her sister to help Kelly, Jake, and you care for him."

Everyone in the family had mourned her mother together, but sometimes Hailey became absorbed in her grief and lost sight of the fact that Rhonda had lost an aunt and her mother had lost her sister. "She agrees with them, then?"

Rhonda's gaze dropped to the barn floor. "I'm so sorry. This has got to be destroying you."

Hailey took another long draw from the beer. "I know Dad's taken Mom's death really hard, but I haven't seen anything that says diminished capacity. It can't be dementia. Can it? He's not that old."

Rhonda let her foot sway back and forth. The heel of her boot occasionally clipped the metal of the gate sounding like an old church bell. The look on her face was one of empathy, but she had no words.

Hailey understood though, even took solace in the silent support of her cousin and best friend. "It is a lot on Kelly and Jake to care for him. Maybe it'd be easier on everybody if I moved home."

"No one expects you to abandon the life you've made

for yourself in the city."

"What life? It's been six weeks since I lost my job, and none of my interviews have panned out. Seems like perfect timing to me."

"The holidays are a really bad time to be looking for a job. You'll get an offer right after the first of the year. I'm sure of it."

Hailey shrugged and set the beer can on the ground. She then stepped up on the bottom rail of the gate, and gripped the top rail, flexing her body and stretching out her back as she used to do when she was younger.

Rhonda began laughing again. "Do not get this thing swinging while I'm sitting on it."

"What's wrong with you? We used do this all the time. Are you too old now?"

"Yes."

Rhonda's simple word rode an infectious giggle. Hailey couldn't help but laugh too. It was always like this when they were together, as if no time had passed, and they were still carefree children.

It was the first time in months she'd been able to smile despite her problems and it felt good to set the weight of the world aside, if only for a few minutes. She hoisted her leg over, and joined her cousin on the gate, facing Rhonda. "But seriously, if I moved back to town, I could help take care of Dad. If it gave him an extra six months at home wouldn't it be worth it?"

Rhonda frowned. "Of course it would, but you don't know that it would give him even an extra day. You need to get all the facts before you make such a big decision. Stop avoiding the conversation with your brother and sister. Sit down and talk to them."

Hailey nodded, gripping the rail in front of her. "I know, you're right."

"I always try to think of New Year's Eve as a big reset button. You'll see. It's time to close the door on all the crap you've gone through the past year and try to face the new one with a bit of hope. You'll get another job."

"I hope your right." Hailey paused and looked up toward the hayloft. "We had so much fun growing up here."

"Didn't your brother catch you up in that hayloft with Jimmy Johnson?"

"Nah! Not Jimmy." Her giggle sounded child-like, even to her own ears.

"Who was it then? I know it wasn't Nate Jenkins. No matter how bad you always wanted it to be."

Hailey pressed her lips together. Some secrets were too precious to speak, even to Rhonda. The incident her cousin remembered wasn't with Nate, but she'd had a moment here with him in the quiet of the old barn too.

It was the Fourth of July the summer before they were all to leave for college. Her parents had encouraged her to have a bonfire with all of her friends from school.

Late in the evening, Nate pulled her aside and asked her to go for a walk and right here—in front of the old gate—he'd asked her out.

"Seems like a hundred years ago."

"You can't go back in time."

"But wouldn't it be nice if we could?"

He'd been so nervous that night. Talked about the weather, the baseball game from TV the night before, and even how high the corn stalks were in the field before he rubbed his sweaty palms on the back of his denim shorts and asked if "she might want to" go out with him.

"What would you do? Not go to college and law school? Marry Nate Jenkins? Work with him in the diner?"

Hailey swung her leg back over the gate and jumped down. With a smooth movement, she reached down, picking up her drink. "Don't say it like that. Nate's a good guy."

"Lighten up. Did I say he wasn't? I'm just saying you made the right choices. That's all."

She leaned her arm against the wall and peeked into an empty stall. "I'm glad *you're* sure. Sometimes I don't know."

"He has a daughter you know."

Hailey nodded. "I heard. He moved home so his mom could help him take care of her when she was a baby. No one knows anything about her mother."

"It's hard to imagine any of us from school with kids of our own. What is she, five?"

"Almost six."

She heard Rhonda's feet hit the ground and then her footfalls. "Really? You're still hung up on him?"

"I didn't say that." Didn't mean it wasn't true though. Hailey turned, leaning back against the wall and facing her cousin. "It's a small town. Jake has actually become pretty good friends with him over the years. I hear things."

"Sounds to me like you're protesting too much."

Hailey shrugged. "I've been thinking a lot about the choices I've made in life. Being out of work gives you a lot of time for introspection."

"Sounds like you've spent too much time examining the past, if you ask me."

"The decision to leave Nate behind and head to college early was huge. Things might have turned out differently if I'd let the rest of the summer play out."

"And things might have turned out differently if my family had left fifteen minutes later or sooner to come over here for Christmas dinner. You'll drive yourself mad thinking about all the 'what ifs.'"

Hailey nodded, crossing her arms in front of her chest. It didn't stop the questions from rolling through her mind. But Rhonda was right about one thing, she couldn't make any decisions based on hypotheses. She needed to gather facts, and her dad's health was a good place to start. "I guess it's time to go have that talk with my brother and sister."

Chapter Two

Nate picked up the last glass out of the soapy water and rinsed it before handing to his daughter. After turning off the faucet and releasing the drain stop, he wiped his hands on the edge of the dishtowel Lori was using to dry the glass.

Thank you for helping, he signed.

Lori put the glass in the cupboard and laid out the towel on the edge of the counter before signing her reply. *I like to help.*

"Hey, quiet down. You two are making such a racket!"

Lori giggled, turning toward the door her aunt had just come through.

"She's pretty silly, huh?" Nate said.

Lori nodded, as Anna picked her up off the chair, and then set her back down on the floor. "Thanks for doing my job for me."

Nate patted his daughter's shoulder. "Why don't you go brush your teeth and pick out a book? I'll be along shortly to read to you."

Lori looped her arms around Anna's waist. "Love you," she whispered.

"Love you too, sweetie," Anna called off to the girl's retreating frame, then turned her attention to Nate. "You fixed such a big meal for just the three of us. Not that I'm complaining—it was wonderful—but we have enough leftovers for a week."

"I did it for Lori," Nate whispered, filling a coffee cup from the pot. He then flipped the switch on the coffee maker and took a seat at the table. "She deserves memorable holidays."

Anna joined him. "She'll remember this Christmas for a long time. Not because it looks like a Toys R Us exploded out there, but because you made the whole day about being with her."

"It is about her. Every day. I'll do anything to see that smile of hers."

Anna shifted her weight in the chair, leaning in a little closer to Nate. "She does have the best smile. And laugh."

"There's nothing else like it, huh?"

Anna pressed her lips tightly together, holding back something she wanted say. Nate knew she wouldn't be able to keep it to herself long. A moment later, she proved him right. "It doesn't help her when you encourage her to sign."

"It doesn't hurt either. In fact, the doctor said it was like learning a second language and showed intelligence that she's been able to pick it up so fast."

"I never equated her speech disorder with a mental deficiency."

If there was one person he could let his defensive walls down around it was sister, but the partition he'd built between Lori, him, and the rest of the town was a comfortable place for him, and protecting his daughter was an automatic reaction. "I know you didn't mean it like that."

"She talks at the barn, you know, because I make her."

"I wish you wouldn't put her in embarrassing situations."

"Her therapist has told you it's not going to get better if she doesn't speak."

"What you've been doing with her and the horses proves that's not true."

"She is responding to hippotherapy but that will only help so much. She needs to converse."

Nate pushed his chair back a few inches from the table and twisted it sideways. He took a deep breath, trying to hold his frustration in check. "I know that. I'm grateful for what her doctor and you've been able to accomplish, but I will not make communicating with my daughter hard. I work with her on her exercises, but we use sign language too."

Anna didn't back down. Not that he expected her to. "I just want what's best for her. For you too."

"You think I don't?"

"I know you do. You'd give her the world if you could. I also think you sometimes encourage the sign language because it makes her dependent on you. It gives the two of you this device for shutting out the rest of the world."

"Well, sometimes the rest of the world sucks. Is it a wonder she doesn't want to talk when the kids at school pick on her for stammering?"

"That happened once or twice, yes, but the teachers dealt with it and it's in the past. I'm not denying the sign language has helped—been a blessing even when her disorder was really bad. All I'm saying is I think you should be actively pushing her to speak. It's the only way it will continue to improve."

Nate nodded, but didn't meet his sister's gaze. He knew she was right on many of her points. Maybe he did hold Lori a little too close sometimes, but wasn't a daddy supposed to protect his little girl?

"We'd be lost without your help." He took a long sip from the coffee mug. "I should get in there and read to her."

Anna reached over and gripped his wrist. "Sit a minute. You deserve a few quiet moments to yourself and you know she could play with those toy ponies you bought her for hours."

"If all goes the way I hope, by spring I might be able to get her that real horse she's been asking for. Jake Lambert says the farm will be available to lease in a few weeks. I just need to figure out how I'm going to squeeze enough money out of my budget to pay what he wants."

"You're really going to do this?"

"It's past time Lori and I got a place of our own."

"When Mom and Dad retired to Arizona they said we could both stay here as long as we wanted. Maybe I should be the one to get a different place?"

Nate fidgeted with the handle of the coffee cup. "It's

about more than leaving this house and having a place that's ours. The therapeutic horse riding has helped her so much, but when she's in school, there aren't enough hours in the day to get her out to Sunnydale. If we move into the Lambert place, I can get her a horse of her own and she'll be able to ride daily."

"If it's going to be a struggle to make the lease, how are you going to afford a horse too?"

He scraped his hand across his jaw. No matter how many times he refigured the budget, he always came up short. "I'll make it work. I have to do what's best for Lori."

"You give her your best every day, with or without a horse of her own." Anna insisted.

"Thanks for saying that."

"It's true." She twisted in the seat and then stood, picking up Nate's now empty coffee cup and taking it to the sink. "It'll be quiet around here without you."

"I'm not moving half way around the world. It's just a mile outside of town. Maybe. If it all works out. I'll still be at the diner every day. I'll still need you to help out with Lori." He leaned back in the chair. "And it won't be until after Bill goes into Pioneer. Probably not until after the first of the year."

Anna turned and leaned back against the counter. "I ran into Kelly at the grocery store the other day. She says Hailey is fighting her and Jake about putting their father in the nursing home."

Hailey. "Is she home?"

"I think Kelly said she was coming in yesterday."

Why after all this time did just hearing that name send him tumbling eight years into the past? After the way she'd treated him, thinking of her should make him angry, or remind him of the pain. Instead, his pulse quickened.

Just as it had when he'd seen her at the beach with her cousin and her cheerleading friends. It was late June and even though there were half a dozen girls in the group deepening their tans and cooling off with occasional dips into the water, he only had eyes for her.

He and his friends from the basketball team crashed the outing. The two groups formed one and they'd spent a few more hours soaking up the sun together before heading across the street to the Dairy Queen.

For him, it'd marked a beginning. She'd been flirty with him, and for the first time he started to believe she might actually be interested in dating him.

But it must have meant more to him than it ever did to her.

"I wonder why she cares. She couldn't wait to get far away from here." *And me.*

Just a couple of weeks after that afternoon and a day after their one and only date, Hailey packed up her car and fled town as fast as she could.

No goodbyes.

That night, he'd thought she returned all the mixed-up feelings he'd felt for her throughout high school. Her rapid exit sent him on a downward spiral.

A feeble attempt to get her out of his mind and heart resulted in the short-term fling that blessed him with his daughter.

Convincing Lori's mother not to put an end to the pregnancy hadn't been easy. Watching the woman walk away from both of them just hours after giving birth had reaffirmed one truth for Nate. He was the kind of guy women easily left.

Over time, Nate accepted the tradeoff. His world revolved around his daughter. She needed him to be there, completely devoted to her needs. He had no spare time to give to a woman who would disregard his daughter and eventually leave him.

"Bill is her dad. Of course she's concerned about his health."

Nate nodded. Anna was right. He shouldn't be questioning Hailey's motives surrounding her father. However, it did seem that once again she was complicating his plan for happiness.

Chapter Three

Didn't it go against some primal law of nature to talk about putting your father in a nursing home on Christmas Day?

Hailey wished they didn't need to have this conversation, but knew it was necessary.

Once the extended family had left, the three siblings gathered in the kitchen. Kelly's husband gave Jake's family a ride home, and Jake would return the favor, dropping his sister off as soon as they'd come to a final decision.

Hailey was glad her father had gone on to bed. She had questions that would be more difficult to ask in front of him and believed his absence would make it easier for her siblings to be candid.

Kelly sat at the head of the kitchen table. Her elbows on the oak surface and her forehead resting against her hands. Her words were drenched with the same sorrow that picked at Hailey's heart. "If you're so against this, are you going to move home to take care of Dad?"

"It's not that I'm against it," Hailey tried to explain. "I just want to be sure it's needed. If moving home would help delay the need, maybe I could. At least for the short term."

Hailey knew a return to Caseville would be viewed by everyone as a step down the corporate ladder, but family was more important than the small town's perception that she'd failed. Even if she kind of, sort of, had. Being unemployed for six weeks wasn't exactly a success story.

"How would that even work?" Jake asked. "You have a job in New York. Besides, I really believe Dad's illness has progressed too far for any of us to manage—even as a team."

"I care about Dad more than any job." Especially a job

she didn't have any more. She asked herself if she'd be offering to do this if she still worked for Cooper, Smith and Bradley. She liked to think the answer would be yes.

"I know you care. We all care. It doesn't change the fact that he really needs around the clock medical attention."

Hailey still wanted to be told of specific incidents that indicated the need. "I know he's getting older and his health is on the decline. But a nursing home? I just don't see how he's reached that point."

Kelly twisted in the chair. "Some days are better than others, and he's strung together a couple of good ones since you've been home. Unfortunately, he's had some bad moments that could have become disastrous if not for well-timed interventions."

Jake paced back and forth in front of the counter. "You're just not seeing a clear picture with your twice a month calls and seasonal trips home. Kelly and I are with him every single day."

"Both of you have homes big enough to take him in."

"And we both have full time jobs," Kelly said. "Besides, my house isn't accessible to him. All my bedrooms are on the second floor."

"You can't turn the kids' play room into a bedroom?"

"He has a hard enough time climbing the two steps into this house, how's he going to manage the broken down stone ones out at my place. I have to think about my kids. He left the stove on last week, you know. He could have burnt the house down."

Hailey moved to the table, sitting next to her sister. She fiddled with the quilted placemat the two of them had made as a Christmas gift for her mother when they were in junior high school. It had adorned the table ever since.

What she'd give for a little of her mother's guidance right now.

"Does that mean he has diminished capacity? You've never started to cook something and got busy? I burnt a grilled cheese sandwich last week. Maybe I should be put in a nursing home too."

Jake bent his knee slightly and leaned back against the refrigerator. "None of us want this."

She turned to her brother. "Then why can't he live with you? Courtney stays home with your kids."

He shook his head. "We talked about that, but with these episodes he's had...I won't put her or the kids in danger."

Hailey narrowed her focus on her brother. She knew her siblings were well intentioned, but couldn't help but wonder if they were exaggerating the truth. "Dad wouldn't hurt anyone."

"You're right. Not the father we grew up with, but a few times now he's become violent when he doesn't remember Mom is gone. I really believe Pioneer Senior Care is the best answer."

As hard as she tried, Hailey couldn't reconcile her siblings' account of the last few months with her memories of the man she idolized. "Maybe I'll take him home with me. I can hire a nurse to care for him while I'm at work."

But can I? It was one thing to stand up for what she believed in, but six weeks without a paycheck was taking a toll. Her severance package was running out too.

Jake crossed his arms in front of his chest and shook his head. "You live on the fourteenth floor of a high rise in a city he knows nothing about. Do you really think Dad would be happier there? I can't see him wandering around a city he doesn't know. No, it's not a good option."

Hailey closed her eyes, hoping to keep back the tears that now pressed against her lids. "You think a nursing home is better than living with family?"

Jake sat next to his sister and patted her hand. "Yes. I do. Pioneer is small. He knows a lot of the staff and we can monitor his care."

"It's still a nursing home."

"He'll be with friends he knows when his mind is firing correctly, and people who will be compassionate when it's not."

"I'm not saying they're bad people but family should care for their own. Isn't that how we were raised? I keep wondering what Mom would say about all of this."

Jake softened. "I hate it too, but I'm sure it's the right decision."

"We're not going to put him there and abandon him," Kelly said. "Larry and I will take the kids to visit. Jake will take his family too."

"Still, I haven't seen any evidence that he's as bad as you say."

Kelly narrowed her gaze. "You think we're lying?"

"I didn't say that. I'm just having trouble processing it all."

Jake squeezed her hand a little tighter. "Like Kelly said, he's had a nice string of good days. I'm sure you'll witness a bad one before long. Trust us, please. Pack up your old room. Let me know what you want sent to your apartment and what you want me to put in storage. The rest we'll give to the Salvation Army."

Hailey looked away from her siblings. Her left knee bounced venting the pent up frustration she was having a hard time communicating. "I'm going on the record as being against selling the farm too."

Kelly stood and walked away from the table. "We're not selling it. Leasing it, for now. The added income will help pay for Dad's care."

"I can pay for it." The moment the words passed her lips, she wanted to reach out and pull them back. She was used to having plenty to live on, but that didn't reflect her current status. Her bank account had nearly disintegrated over the last six weeks, but they didn't know that and now wasn't the time to tell them.

Besides, she'd find work right after the holidays and rebuild her bank account without dipping into her savings too much.

Jake shook his head and took a sudden interest in his shoes. "That's not right. We'll split it among the three of us. Besides, I'd rather have someone here, keeping up the property. It's better than it sitting empty."

The image of strangers living in her house ran through Hailey's mind and she bristled. "But it's our house."

"A house you rarely visit," Jake said.

"Do you think any of this is easier just because I'm not here day in and day out?"

"Yes, I do. You've already made a break from here," Kelly said.

She'd had goals and done what was necessary to achieve them.

The family didn't need to know she was beginning to regret some of the things that ambition had cost her. "You're wrong, you know. This is tearing me apart."

Jake pushed the chair back and found his feet. "Just do me a favor. Really watch Dad the next few days and keep in mind what we've said. We can talk again tomorrow."

Chapter Four

Hailey stood at the back door watching until her brother's SUV reached the end of the driveway and made the left turn onto the road.

Even though she knew it wasn't in either Kelly or Jake's characters to exaggerate or abandon family, she still had a hard time coming to terms with the picture they painted for her.

Jake was right, though. At the very least, she was here for the week. They could take a day or two for Hailey to really observe her father for herself.

She traversed up the steps and down the hall to her bedroom, nearly tripping over three new totes. Jake—or maybe Kelly's husband Larry—must have brought them down from the attic while she was out in the barn with Rhonda.

Dropping down to the bed, she cursed aloud. Jake had said he'd give her time to come to terms, but his actions still screamed that the decision had been made, whether she liked it or not.

Hailey pinched the bridge of her nose, trying to fend off the building stress headache. Was it too much to ask to not have to pack up her father's house during the holidays?

Living alone, so far away from the people she loved had left a hollow pit inside her. The emptiness had forced her to examine her life with a magnifying glass: why wasn't she happy? How had her choices brought her here? Where had she gone wrong?

She had been good at her job; only lost it because she'd stood up to her bosses in defense of a client. A client they had told her to drop because there was no money to be had.

Looking back, she realized the work she'd done in the

firm just hadn't fulfilled her as she'd thought it would.

It was far too early and she was much too conflicted to go to sleep. She retrieved the rubber tote from the top of the stack, took it back toward the bed, and placed it on the floor before making herself comfortable on the patchwork quilt that covered the twin mattress. As she pulled off the lid, the smell of mothballs hit her senses and she turned her face away, closing her eyes. No wonder moths avoided the clothes packed up with them, any one or thing with a sense of smell would.

Her stomach twisted into a knot. Funny how something that smelled so awful could make her miss her mother so much. Every season, the clothes that wouldn't be needed for several months were packed up and put in the attic. When they were brought back down, they'd need to be washed twice to get rid of the smell.

Her cheerleading uniform was draped on the top. She pulled it aside, finding her track uniform. Memories flooded over her and a smile lifted the corners of her mouth.

Accolades for academic achievement and a handful of debate trophies—the small ones, third place or lower—filled the rest of the tote. The big ones were probably still displayed in the glass cabinet in Mr. Tucker's classroom. He'd been the first one to label her a star. A true mentor, he'd put the bug in her ear about the bigger world that lay beyond the boundaries of town.

She made a mental note to look him up before she went home, and reached for her old backpack. Bright and bold in her high school's colors of red and black with the eagle mascot screened on the back, it was a memory of high school she hadn't wanted to take with her to college. She opened the zipper to the main pouch, frowning when there was no forgotten treasure to rediscover.

I'll give it to one of Kelly's kids.

She tossed it aside, and it made a funny crunchy noise when it hit the tote lid.

Hailey picked it back up, examining the front pocket. She pulled out a greeting card size envelope. Once white, now yellowed by time, it bore a name written in blue balloon letters.

Nate Jenkins.

He was never really too far out of her mind or heart, but since crossing the city limits the day before, he'd been all she could think about.

She opened the envelope and dumped the contents on the bed: about two dozen newspaper clippings recording Nate's high school basketball career, and a handful of photographs.

There was one from the putt-putt course across from the beach taken spring break of their junior year. Another was during the karaoke contest, part of the Cheeseburger Festival events that summer between junior and senior year. After that, the group of friends had all come back to her house—including Nate—and had a large bonfire, somewhat of an annual tradition among the Lambert kids.

She carefully flipped through the frail pieces of paper, now remembering how she'd shoved the envelope into her backpack and then hid it in the closet before leaving.

Her mother must have later packed everything into the totes and moved it to the attic.

After that night in the back of Nate's truck, she'd spent the next day avoiding his calls and convincing her mother to let her go spend the last month of her summer vacation with Rhonda in Saginaw before heading on to college in New York City.

It'll be easier to shop for school in the city.

I won't get another chance to see Rhonda for a long time.

I just want to go.

She'd used those arguments and dozens more, never once admitting the truth to her parents. How could she tell them that if she spent the next four weeks as she had the evening before—in Nate's arms—leaving the small town would become impossible?

Everyone was so proud of her for getting the full ride scholarship to New York University. Teachers had written letters of recommendation. Her parents had scraped together the money to pay for housing. Even newly married Jake had contributed some cash so she could buy the Ford Escort that had carried her out of town.

Each of them had such big expectations for her future but none loftier than the goals she'd set for herself.

Giving it all up for Nate would have disappointed so many, and when she entertained the thought of doing just that, Hailey knew she had to take action before the desires of her heart let down everyone around her.

Her eyes locked on her favorite picture. One of her, Nate, and two of his friends all sitting on the tailgate of his truck. Looking at his easy smile and the way he leaned back on his elbows with his head tipped toward hers made her question those choices again.

She slid off the bed and walked toward the door, sliding the picture into the corner of the mirror. Letting her fingers graze over his face, she remembered the way his cheek felt against her hand, the scent of the beach and his Axe cologne clouded her senses.

If she could click her heels together and go back to that moment in time, would she make different choices?

A loud slamming door pulled Hailey back from the recent past. She went into the hallway, calling her father's name.

"Diane!" he called out.

Her mother. Panic froze Hailey's feet to the floor for a split second. Was this one of those moments?

She hit the bottom of the staircase as her father came around the corner from the kitchen. She touched his shoulders and looked into his eyes. "Are you okay?"

He squinted at her like a lost child before despair took over his features.

"Hailey! Where's your mother? I don't know where she's at."

She swallowed hard and reached out, taking his hand. "She's gone, Dad. Remember?"

He tipped his chin. Confusion clouded his eyes. "Gone where? It's the middle of the night."

"Dad," Hailey whispered, then took a deep breath and focused. She needed to do this without emotion. "She died. Last summer. Remember?"

He shook his head and took a step back. The shock on his face was like a knife to her chest. "Of course I remember." He spit his words before turning back toward the kitchen.

She followed him, wanting to find a way to ease the tension and his confusion. "What do you say? Why don't I make us some hot chocolate?"

"Don't go to the trouble." Still belligerent. So foreign from the dad of her youth.

"It's not."

"I'd rather have you sit with me." He took his regular seat at the head of the table. She answered his request and joined him. "I miss your mother."

"Me too."

"Never get old. It isn't much fun."

She twisted her body toward him and painted on a smile, hoping she could lighten the mood. "It's better than the alternative, don't you think?"

He chuckled. "Yeah, yeah, I guess you're right."

It felt awkward to be silent in the same room with her father. Still, finding the right words proved impossible.

Thankfully, he found words to fill the void. "I was looking at the old barn this afternoon. From the hayloft, I noticed a soft spot in the roof. I'm going to have to see if I can get your brother up there to have a look."

Trying to ignore the fact her elderly father had climbed up into the hayloft, she forced herself to concentrate on his concern. The barn hadn't held animals since Hailey's last 4-H project. Two of her uncles still farmed the land, but they used their own buildings for storage. The haven of her youth was now deserted and showing its age.

"I was out there with Rhonda tonight. I didn't notice a problem with the roof."

"I figured that's where the two of you ran off to. Could never keep you girls out of there when you were young."

"We could have been doing a lot worse than playing in the hay or riding the gate."

"You're absolutely right about that. That's why we have to keep it up. Yes. I'm going have to climb up there tomorrow and see what I need to fix it."

Reaching across the table, she squeezed his hand. "Please. Promise me you won't do that. I'll talk to Jake. And we'll make sure we get it fixed. I don't want you to get hurt."

"All these years, I've always maintained the property on my own." Sadness replaced the pride that had shown in his eyes. "It really stinks that I've gotten so damn old I can't take care of things anymore."

"You shouldn't have to. We kids are old enough now. Let us pick up the slack."

He leveled his hard gaze on her. "No matter what happens to me, I want that barn maintained. There's too much development going on around here. Too much change."

The plea in her father's voice nipped at her heart, but didn't resemble the frail and forgetful father Jake and Kelly had warned her about. He wasn't even the same man who stood before her like a confused child five minutes ago.

Sure, he'd been looking for her mother, but she'd lost count of the number of times she'd reached for her phone and dialed home before remembering her mom was gone.

Seeing the desperation in her father's eyes, she knew any extra day she could give her father in this house would be worth it.

"I promise, Dad." She eased back into the chair. "Remember Polly?"

Her father laughed. "Remember her? That stupid pony nipped at me last week. I swear the ol' girl is more mule than horse."

"Aunt Iva and Uncle Ray still have her?"

Bill nodded. "She carried you around the ring for how many years, and then your cousins, now Ray's grandkids are showing her."

Her jaw dropped. "Really? Showing her?"

"Absolutely. She shows her age, of course. We all do. They can't jump her over fences anymore, but she still shines like a diamond in the showmanship classes."

"Amazing!" She leaned back in the chair, twisting a lock of hair around her finger. This moment had been repeated so many times over the years. Heart to hearts with her dad at the kitchen table had helped her through many a problem—both big and small. The idea that everything was going to change—that it might be someone else's family sitting at this table next Christmas nipped at her heart like her pony used to bite at her hand.

She'd always felt comfort in the knowledge that she could come home.

Pioneer Senior Care wasn't home.

Chapter Five

Nate slid the dollar bills and quarters that were scattered on the counter top together and then pulled them to the edge. When the extra cash was safely in the pocket of his apron, he picked up the now empty coffee cups and dropped them in the bus pan near the kitchen door.

During the busier times he worked side-by-side with the other cook, but at this time of the morning he covered the counter while two waitresses handled the floor.

"Need another refill, Jake?" He asked the last of his early-morning, regular customers.

"No. Thanks anyway. I need to head out to Dad's. Kelly and I made some progress convincing Hailey that Dad needs to move into Pioneer, but she's still resistant."

"She doesn't want you to rent me the property?"

"I haven't told her you were interested in it yet. She doesn't even want to put Dad in a nursing home."

"Really?"

"She just isn't around enough to see how bad he's become. His good days are really good."

"And the bad days are really bad?"

Jake's only response was to nod.

Nate had seen the rapid decline in Bill Lambert's health for himself. Just a few weeks ago, he'd come into the diner for lunch. After ordering, he became so disoriented that Nate had to call Jake's wife to come pick him up. Nate suspected that the younger Lamberts and taken Bills keys that day, because he hadn't been seen in town alone since.

Nate knew it was unlikely but asked anyway. "Is she thinking about moving home to care for him?"

Jake drummed his fingers against the counter. "I wouldn't think so, but she did suggest it last night." After a brief pause, he sat up a little straighter. "Don't worry. Give her a few more days to see the situation for what it is and she'll know we're right. Then she'll go back to New York, and we can move forward with leasing the farm."

"She really can't see how far your dad has slipped away the past few months?"

Jake shook his head. "She says we're being unfair. Thinks we're just trying to stuff him away somewhere." Jake's shoulders fell, his chest deflated. "You know, I wish Hailey was right. I hate seeing my father like this. The last thing I want to do is put him in a nursing home. I wouldn't if I didn't believe it was our only option."

"I know that."

"You wouldn't want to talk to Hailey and tell her I'm right. Would you?"

Good question. Could Nate have a conversation with her and not tumble back into their twisted past? The color must have drained from his face, because Jake laughed.

"I'm kidding."

Maybe so, but Jake's half-hearted request had forced Nate to realize that renting the Lambert farm might translate to having to deal with Hailey. She'd been avoiding him for eight years now. What made him think she would okay the deal he and Jake had hammered out? "I'm very interested in renting the house, but I don't want to get in the middle of a family fight."

"It's not a fight. Hailey just needs some time to get used to the idea. Dad's moving into Pioneer right after the first of the year, then we'll work out the details of our plan." Jake stood and fished his wallet out of his back pocket.

Nate looked over his shoulder to the street and then glanced back at his watch. It wasn't unusual for there to be a lull in business between the early morning crowd and the late morning rush. The week between Christmas and New Year was typically slow, but Nate couldn't stop worrying.

Ever since they had started negotiating about the house, Nate had been counting every customer and figuring the profit margin on every order.

The columns of numbers he'd been studying way past midnight flashed in his mind again. No matter how he tried to arrange them or cut costs, it still didn't make fiscal sense to do what his daughter needed him to do. Coming up with rent was going to be hard enough but—eventually—he hoped to buy the farm.

If he wanted the bank to give him a mortgage on the house, it was imperative that he keep the restaurant in the black, something he had successfully done since taking it over two years before, but that was before the business had to support a lease on a farm.

Jake threw a ten-dollar bill on the counter and folded up the newspaper, tucking it under his arm. "We're good. I don't need change. You should give the wife a call. My girls would love to have Lori over to play while they're off school."

"Thanks. I'll do that." A polite response. Nate believed that Jake meant the offer. He'd always been a good friend and never seemed to be bothered or affected by all the rumors surrounding Nate and his daughter. Lori, however, wouldn't be comfortable with a play date. The only ones she really communicated with were Anna, him, and the horses.

Regular meetings with her principal, teachers, and counselors had resulted in all of them learning sign language, or at least enough that Lori could communicate with the adults.

The kids were another story. They didn't know, nor did they want to learn sign language, and Lori's teachers often reported that she was introverted in class. No, he wouldn't be putting undue stress on his daughter by forcing a play date, no matter how sincere Jake's offer was.

Jake turned toward the door but then leaned back against the stool. Nate followed his gaze and saw Hailey approaching. Her hand on her father's elbow, she carefully guided him. Apparently Jake didn't think she could handle the task. He tossed the newspaper to the counter behind him, crossing toward the door. "What in the world does she think she's doing?"

Nate swallowed the lump forming in his throat. Even with all the effort of helping the elderly man, Hailey looked as striking as he remembered. Her straight, blonde hair brushed her shoulders. A pulled snug sash at the waist of her brown suede jacket accented her tone figure. "It looks like she's taking your dad out to breakfast."

"If he loses his footing on the sidewalk, she's not strong enough to keep him from falling. He's going to get hurt." As they approached the door, Jake pushed it open and reached out for his father's other arm. "Be careful, Dad. The sidewalk is slick right here." He then looked to his sister. "This is a surprise."

"I decided to treat Dad to pancakes."

"The roads are pretty slippery, what with all the snow we got last night."

"We get snow in New York, too. I haven't forgotten how to drive in it." She was much shorter than her brother, but Hailey held her chin up and defended her position.

"Your sister managed the roads just fine." Bill interrupted them in the same way he probably did when they were toddlers. He then called out to Nate. "Can you bring me and my daughter some coffee, please?"

Something about having her step out of his fantasies and into his diner, made Nate's palms start to sweat. Words failed to form, and he nodded.

Bill turned to his son. "Join us for breakfast?"

"I just finished up, but I'll sit down and have some coffee with you. I was actually on my way out to your place."

After her father sat, Hailey looked around the restaurant, briefly making eye contact with Nate before turning back to her brother. "I'll be right back. I left my phone in the car." She made a hasty exit, slipping on the sidewalk as she turned to go up the street.

"Let me tell you something," Bill said after the door closed. "Your sister never stops working. She's had her head buried in her computer or been on the phone all morning. I was hoping we'd get some peace and quiet while we ate."

"We all work hard, Dad. The mill is shut down this week, but normally I work ten hours a day."

Nate filled three mugs and set them on a tray along with a pitcher of fresh cream. After placing the cups on the table, he ambled over to the large window looking in the direction Hailey had gone in such a rush.

He could see her on her phone in the small sports car. She ran her fingers through her hair and flipped through pages of notes, looking more rattled than he'd ever remembered seeing her.

Life had changed for the both of them since graduation, but hers had stayed on track. Or at least that's what he'd picked up from bits and pieces of overheard conversations.

When Nate looked back, he was reminded that precious gifts often came wrapped in tragedy. At least that's how it worked out for him. Now, the one person who was blocking his new road to happiness was the same one who had turned his life upside down eight years ago.

So why would he give just about anything to kiss her again? Or at least talk to her and find out why he hadn't been worth a goodbye.

"Nate," Bill called out. "Can we get another round of coffee?"

"Of course."

"And why don't you go ahead and order?" Jake said. "Who knows how long Hailey is going to be out on the phone."

It was fifteen minutes later when Nate was delivering a daily breakfast special to Bill—which ironically did not include pancakes—that Hailey came back into the diner.

"Find your phone?" Jake asked.

Hailey held it up before dropping it to the table. "I had to deal with an important call."

She looked up at Nate briefly. When their eyes met, she just as quickly looked away. "Can I get a bowl of oatmeal, please?"

Nate knew laughing was inappropriate but couldn't keep himself from doing it. "I thought you two wanted my world famous pancakes?"

Hailey flipped her attention to her father's plate and then back again. "You know what, you're right. How often do I get the chance to eat pancakes from the Front Porch? Bring that."

"Sure thing," Nate said. "And I'll warm up your coffee too, just as soon as I get the Perkins' order."

Nate moved back to the counter and tried to focus on the couple's breakfast requests. Not an easy task given the way his head was swimming.

Just floating with the motion of the waves, as they had done that day at the beach. In reality it might have been a group of friends enjoying their last summer before college. In his mind, it had become a first real date, and the prelude to the following night. That last night he'd spent any real time with her, or had anything that even resembled a conversation.

While his emotions were twisted into knots, calm, cool, and collected Hailey didn't show even a hint of regret or remorse. Did she ever think of him and the one night that still burned in his heart? It didn't appear so.

****

Hailey hadn't exactly lied when she said the phone call had been important. It was her landlord inquiring about the late payment on her lease. She'd been hoping to hold him off another week but relented and gave him her credit card number over the phone.

The job prospects would be better after the first of the year. They sure couldn't get any worse. Once she had a new job, she could tell her family the whole story about the last couple of months. Until then, she'd keep the pasted smile on her face; let them believe she was still the all-in-control girl they thought she was.

Several people, all with familiar faces, had entered the diner while she'd been in the car, and she felt a little more

34

at ease.

Being in the same room with Nate stung more than she thought it would. The ache in her heart was as strong as the day she'd hastily thrown her things into that old Escort and driven toward the city as fast as the beat-up car would take her.

She tried to keep her focus on her family—struggled to follow her brother's conversation with her father—but couldn't keep her eyes from wandering back to Nate. He laughed with his customers and staff and then turned the orders into the kitchen.

A tapping noise snapped her attention back to her brother. He glared at her while he drummed his fingers on the table. "Am I boring you?"

She shook away the cobwebs. "I'm sorry. What were you saying?"

"Kelly is going to come sit with Dad this afternoon so we can go over to Pioneer. I want you to take a tour. Maybe that will ease your mind."

How could Jake be talking like this in front of their father, as if his feelings didn't matter and he didn't have a say? She refused to disrespect their dad and spoke to him instead of her brother. "Do you understand what Jake and Kelly want to do?"

Her dad nodded slightly, avoiding her gaze. "It's okay. They think this is for the best."

"What do you want?"

"To not be a burden on any of you."

"You're no such thing. I would love to have you come live with me." That was, if she could get a job and hold on to her apartment.

Her brother shifted his weight in the chair and leaned forward to speak. Her father beat him to it. "It means a lot to me that you would ask, but it's a bad idea."

She swallowed hard. "Why do you think that?"

"Because you work very long hours. I would be away from everyone and everything I know. Jake, Kelly and I have talked about Pioneer. I understand."

"I'm not so sure they're right on this one."

He set his fork next to his plate, and stared at the utensils like they were foreign objects. The emptiness that resided in his eyes the night before returned. "But, I've been lonely. I miss your momma."

"We all miss her."

"I don't remember things like I used to. I get confused from time to time."

"That's part of getting older. There has to be things we can do to help you. Maybe we could make lists and post them up on the refrigerator."

Jake jumped in. "Really? You think a big to-do list is the answer to his medical illness? If you're not going to be here to help manage this situation, I need you to step back."

Hailey tried to ignore her brother's words, even though his complaints hurt. She worked to make eye contact with her dad, difficult because he wouldn't lift his stare from the table. "Why are you afraid to tell him how you feel about the house? Tell Jake what you told me last night, about wanting the farm to stay the same."

Her father touched his fingers to his temples and closed his eyes, shaking his head.

"Stop this!" Jake said. "Can't you see you're upsetting him?"

"Me?"

Standing, Jake took his father's elbow. Despite being visibly unnerved, Jake spoke with a softness reserved for a small child. "Come on, Dad. Let me take you home."

Hailey leapt to her feet too. Her father turned to her, holding his hand up. "Stop. Please. Your brother knows how to handle these situations."

"What situations? We're just talking."

She could see his hands were trembling and his eyes flickered back and forth. "I'm going with Jake. I want you to do what he asks."

Before Hailey could respond Jake did with a firm but level voice. "Let me take him home. Eat your breakfast, get a hold of your emotions, and then come to the house so we can have a rational conversation about this."

She stepped back, and dropped down to the chair. *Rational conversation?* She'd thought that's what they were doing, until everything spun three hundred and sixty degrees without warning.

Only when she heard the bell above the door ring out, was she able to unclench her fists and let out the breath that had tightened her chest. She'd seen Nate lingering around the edge of the counter with her plate of pancakes in hand but didn't want him to approach her now.

She really didn't have it in her to deal with him.

He came forward anyway, and set the plate in front of her. After a hesitation, he asked, "Can I sit for a minute?"

Her eyes fluttered closed, but she gestured to the chair. She heard it scrape against the old worn tile and could feel him just inches away from her.

"I'm sorry your dad's health is on the decline. I've always really liked him. It stinks, you know."

She took a deep breath; maybe they could talk as old friends and ignore the complications of the night they'd spent together. "I don't think he's that bad. Jake and Kelly are overreacting."

He twisted his hands on his lap. "I can see how you would think that. Some days when I see him, he's sharp as nails. Others...."

Her phone vibrated against the table. The habit to check the ID won out against the desire to meet Nate's stare. An eight-hundred number flashed, twisting Hailey's stomach into knots. Another bill collector wanting to take the money she was trying to stretch just a little further, hoping to get through a few more weeks. She hit the button to ignore the call.

"I overheard what you said about your dad wanting the property to stay the same," Nate said. "I'll take real good care of the place and won't change a thing. I love that farm the way it is."

That brought her attention back. "What are you talking

about?"

"I've been talking to Jake about renting the house."

She took in his deep brown eyes and almost black hair. It was cropped short like he was trying to beat-the-heat, even if the average temperature this week was somewhere around ten degrees. Much shorter than he wore it in high school. The neatly trimmed beard and mustache were new too.

He looked older. More settled.

How ironic.

They'd both thought this small town would smother them back then.

For a fleeting moment it comforted her to picture Nate cooking in her family's kitchen, and then she realized it wouldn't be her house anymore. She'd be on the outside looking in. "It feels like everything is being taken away from me."

His body stiffened as he pulled back. "It's not like I'm stealing it. I'm going to pay you for it."

"This isn't about money!"

"Then what is it about?"

She reached for her purse and fumbled for her wallet with trembling hands. "Everyone seems to think that just because I don't live here, I don't have a voice, but you're all wrong." She threw a twenty-dollar bill on the table. "I didn't leave the planet, I moved to New York. I didn't abandon my family, but it feels like they think so. I'm sick of being treated like an outside in my hometown, in my family home, in my own life."

She stood and tried to turn, but he grabbed her wrist. Looking back would weaken her resolve—Nate had always had that effect on her—but she did it anyway.

"Please, it would mean a lot to Lori…and me."

His daughter. The child he'd had with someone else. She couldn't stand the thought of the two of them in her living room without her.

Why did it hurt so much?

It wasn't as if he left her. She'd pursued and claimed

the future she'd always wanted.

Hadn't she?

If everything she'd attained had been all she ever wanted, why was it tearing her in two to know Nate had gone on with his life without her? It wasn't as if she'd expected he wouldn't. She should be happy he was settled. Instead, it made her long for that place next to him even more.

A lump formed in her throat, making speech impossible. Instead, she headed for the door.

"That's right, Hailey. Run away. It's what you do best!"

His words stopped her, and she twisted back. "I what?"

"Run. Away. When the pieces of your life don't come together like a neat little puzzle, you scatter them all around you and stomp out of the room."

She bristled at the venom in his voice. "That's not what happened."

"Oh, no. You handled it so well, just breezed out of town with no concern for those you left behind."

They weren't talking about her father or her house anymore. This was about how she'd reacted eight years ago, when the feelings got too real.

Just as they were now.

"I care, dammit!" She let out a long exhale. "I always have."

Chapter Six

Lori snored lightly against Nate's chest, signaling that she'd fallen asleep. He closed the book and let it rest on his lap. Taking a moment to collect his thoughts, he leaned back against the headboard.

Like a hundred other times since seeing Hailey in the diner, his mind rolled back to his senior year and how enamored he'd been with her. How horribly smitten and how completely invisible to her. Until that one wonderful day and incredible night.

It had started with dinner at the pizzeria. Now, he could give his teenaged self a swift kick for not reaching for something more special, but at the time it seemed perfect. And if Hailey thought he'd gone for cheap, she never let on that night.

Dinner was followed by a movie before they raided the dessert case in the already closed diner. Even later, they parked in his truck down on the deserted beach.

As he lived through that night, he was sure it was the beginning of something special…at least for the few weeks of summer they had left before embarking to separate colleges. There hadn't been clue one those few hours were to be the beginning, middle and end of them as a couple.

He'd spent numerous times over the years, looking back, thinking about choices made and roads taken. When times got tough, he wondered if his life would have turned out differently if Hailey hadn't left town early.

If only she'd let the rest of the summer play out.

Would he have ended up following her to New York? Would she have given up her full ride to go to college with him? Maybe they'd have had a good time and gone their separate ways in the fall.

He knew the questions were impossible to answer.

Before, he'd been able to entertain them for a time and then sweep them under a rug.

But not today.

This morning, strong-willed Hailey had met him head on, and when things didn't fall into their perfect little place for her, she ran. Again.

The last words he'd said to her slipped past his lips before he could stop them. Part of him felt lighter having confronted her. Even if he'd been a little childish and somewhat passive-aggressive.

Another piece of his heart felt guilty when she froze in her tracks. She'd turned and argued against his accusations. And then, her final words had hit him in the chest like a knife.

She'd always cared. Surely, she meant about her parents, her family, and their farm.

Shaking it all away, he leaned over and kissed his daughter's forehead, refusing to curse the missteps of his past. Each one led him to this moment and he was happy with his life. He wouldn't change a thing if the result meant he didn't have Lori.

Maybe that confrontation in the diner would give him the strength to close the door to all those questions.

Placing a foot on the floor, Nate slipped off the edge of the twin bed and smoothed the quilt out over his daughter. Making sure he dimmed the light to a low, golden amber, he left her door open just a crack.

After turning on the Christmas tree lights, he settled down in his favorite chair in front of the fireplace. Hoisting his leg up on the footstool, he tried to decide if he'd be awake long enough to warrant building a fire. His body was exhausted, but his mind was running in circles. He decided against it, even though sleep would probably elude him.

He opened the drawer on the end table next to his chair, pulling out his sketchbook and a piece of charcoal vine. Flipping through the pages of his recent drawings, he longed to see the passion that used to exist in his work. Even the most recent sketches of his daughter had a flat

41

quality about them that he couldn't figure out how to remedy.

Turning to a blank page, he leaned back in his chair and studied the tree. He looked at the lines of the branches and the orbs of bulbs and lights, studied the contrast of light and dark. Then, he turned to his book and began putting those lines and shadows on the page.

A career that used his artistic talents was a distant memory, an abandoned road that he didn't lament. Quite the opposite, he turned to his sketchbooks or canvases to bleed his emotions or dissolve his stress.

Noticing the way he'd naturally divided the page into halves, both horizontally and vertically, he turned his focus to the upper left, empty quadrant. He touched the end of the charcoal to the paper and closed his eyes waiting for inspiration to strike. His first thought—*Hailey*—flashed through his brain. He tried to push it away. In the same way she'd fought back with him in the diner that morning, her images remained. He opened his eyes and exorcised those demons the only way he knew, by spilling them onto the page.

The curve of her face. The way her hair framed her cheeks and touched her shoulders. Her full lips and round eyes. They all bled from his memory to the page with an ease that was unnerving to him.

When he finished he was amazed by the likeness he'd created, especially since it all came from memory.

A pair of headlights flashed through the west window shaking his attention from the sketch and pulling him back into the real world.

Just as they were sitting down to dinner, Anna had been called back to the stable because a horse had colic. Lori had begged to go help, but he'd denied the request, thinking the horse's treatment would continue long into the night. He was pleased for his sister and for the horse that he'd been wrong.

If Anna was already home, it couldn't have been serious. Knowing she would be hungry, he made his way to the kitchen to warm up the plate he'd set aside for her.

A heavy knock on the front door signaled it was someone else, so he put the plate back in the refrigerator.

In the front entry, he flipped on the porch light and then pulled the worn, lime green curtain aside. Under the soft yellow glow, stood Hailey.

Light fluffy snow blew from the roof, cascading around her. She looked like a delicate flower—one that would whither in the cold—her hands were pushed into the pockets of the same suede coat she'd worn earlier. The dark brown scarf hung over her shoulders untied. And she was staring up where the Christmas lights hung off the edge of the roof.

Sad didn't properly describe the way she looked. It went deeper than that.

Surprising, given how hot she'd been when she stomped out of the diner. What shocked him more was his first desire: to slide his fingers under her chin, lift her mouth toward him, and kiss her.

Just one more time.

He dug deep for resolve, reminding himself she stood in the way of him taking possession of the farm. She wasn't here for a walk down memory lane or to rekindle the smoldering embers of his heart.

She was most likely here to state yet again why she didn't want to let go of the farm. Why she'd rather see it sit empty then let him and Lori live there.

He readied himself to stand tall against her and then pulled open the door. "What do you want?"

She shook her head, opened her mouth to speak, and then clamped it shut. The edge of her mouth turned down and she twisted the heel of her boot against the concrete. "You're wrong about me."

The words he understood, but not her tone. She sounded absolutely miserable. "What are you talking about?"

"What you said in the diner. About me always running away. That's not fair."

He reclaimed the ground between them he'd relinquished. Pushing open the screen door, he stepped onto the porch. "Do you remember things differently than I do?"

Her chest heaved and she tipped her chin to the right.

A tinge of guilt pinged at Nate when he saw just how his words had penetrated Hailey's shell.

She'd ripped his heart out all those years ago, but the idea that he'd hurt her cut at him. It didn't change the way he felt about their past but the desire to take her in his arms—comfort her—bubbled up again.

"We were young." She started down the steps, but paused at the bottom, turning back. "I made some very stupid choices and I'm sorry for that."

An apology had been the last thing he expected when he'd seen her standing on the porch and while it probably should have been enough, it wasn't. Instead, it only opened more questions about the past. "You came all the way over here to tell me that?"

Hailey slid her hand through her hair, pulling it off her face and shaking her head. "No. But then I saw you and...well...we were both a lot younger then."

Nate fought the urge to laugh. It wasn't funny that she was so conflicted, but ironic that he wasn't the only one haunted by the past. It seemed it had them both hanging in the wind.

They needed to talk it out if they were to ever move forward. He reached out and took her elbow. "Come in out of the snow. I'll make a pot of coffee."

She accepted the invitation. After slipping off her coat, she handed it to him, before stepping over the threshold and heading for the couch.

Nate ran his fingers over the suede. It was as soft as he'd imagined it would be. He hung it on the coat tree and then peeked around the corner. Hailey had made herself comfortable in the living room, as if she'd been here a thousand times before.

In his dreams, she had.

Just moments ago, angst had her fleeing for her car. Now, her eyes flickered back and forth between the tree and him.

"How do you like your coffee?"

She tapped the cushion next to her. "Please. I don't want you to wait on me. That's not why I came."

A piece of him wanted to be compassionate, sit next to her and tell her it was okay, that he was glad she was here. He set that aside; reminded himself not to get mesmerized by her.

He had to stand tall, for Lori. If Hailey didn't let him move into her father's house, his daughter wouldn't get what she needed to improve her speech. "Then why did you come?"

"To talk."

"But not about the past?" Again the words of his heart slipped past his lips before his brain had the chance to censor them. It felt good to unload the burdens he'd been harboring, but when she rebuffed him by turning her head and closing her eyes, regret filled the space vacated in his chest.

"I didn't mean to hurt you. Back then, I mean."

So, they were really going to talk about this. He crossed to his chair and sat down. "It was a long time ago. A lot has happened... for both of us."

She gave him a slight nod. "I really came to talk to you about Dad and the house. I want you to know that I'm not angry at you, just the situation."

He felt the tension drain from his shoulders. What she was going through had to be hard. No matter how much it hurt to look at her now, he didn't get joy from what she'd had to deal with in the last year. "I understand this is hard for you. I can't imagine being in your shoes and having to come to terms with one of my parents getting too old to care for themselves—"

"That's the thing, I don't believe he is. He might not be as sharp as he was five or six years ago, but—"

"Were you even in the diner today? Couldn't you see

him slipping away?"

She gripped her chin, shaking her head just a bit. "I don't know. I guess. He got a little confused with me too, but I haven't seen anything with my own to eyes yet that has confirmed for me he can't take care of himself."

He could see she was struggling, but just because she hadn't seen it, didn't mean the events hadn't happened. "Did Jake tell you about him getting disoriented in the diner a few weeks ago?"

She nodded. "And it's not that I don't believe you or Jake. I just have this little voice inside me telling me it's wrong to put Dad in a nursing home."

"I think you would see things differently if you were here every day."

"Maybe you're right. That's my point. Maybe it's the lawyer in me, but I want to see it with my own eyes, or have something that convinces me it's the right step to take. I want to know in my heart he can't take care of himself, and I haven't had any of that happen yet."

"I think that's a little naive."

"Excuse me?"

"Unfortunately, life isn't about a collection of easy choices and flat paved roads. There are ups and downs. We get banged up and scratched. And the right choices are sometimes the most difficult to make."

"I'm sorry for what I did back then."

He hadn't been talking about the past, but when she apologized yet again, he realized what he said fit the moment. "You've said that. A few times now."

"I mean it. And I don't always run away."

"Maybe I shouldn't have said that." Truth. It had felt good to call Hailey out on her inability to face him. But, being right didn't justify kicking her while life had laid her out on her butt. "I was frustrated. Jake says your father is going into Pioneer. He and Kelly need to lease out the property to help pay for his care. I need to get a house outside of town with enough space to get my daughter a horse. This arrangement is a perfect answer to all our problems."

"So I should stand by and put my dad in a nursing home so you can get your kid a horse?"

Nate couldn't just sit in the chair and take it anymore. He found his feet. "You're living in a dream world. You always have. Even I can see how much your father's health has declined since your mother died. Now, I can totally get why you wouldn't *want* to see that, but the only one you're hurting by not facing the truth is your dad. *And* my kid. Mess up your family all you want, but I'll be damned if I just step aside and let you hurt mine."

"Daddy!" Lori's shrill voice cut through the room, so loud it seemed to rattle the windows.

Nate turned and started for the hall but twisted back to Hailey. He spoke with determination. "Do not leave! We're not done, yet."

Lori was sitting up in bed, her eyes squeezed shut and her hands clutching the quilt. She screamed for him again, rocking back and forth.

He pushed a knee to the side of the bed and leaned over her, wrapping his arms around her neck. "Shhh. It's okay."

The nightmares weren't new. She'd been having them regularly for nearly a year and a half. They started about the same time his parents moved out and retired to Arizona. About the same time her stammering had started.

Before that, Nate had shared the bedroom with Lori. He'd just begun looking for a place for the two of them—citing that Lori was getting too old to have to share a room with her father—when his parents announced their plans to move out west.

His father's emphysema had been growing worse—still Nate suspected they'd pushed ahead their plans to move to a warmer, drier climate to make things easier on him. Either way, Lori's social circle had been cut in half.

The grandparents she'd adored were gone. As her speech deteriorated, phone conversations grew impossible. The less contact she had with them, the more frequent the nightmares had become.

"Daddy's here, baby. Take a deep breath."

She opened her eyes and the terror that had been on her face melted to something different. She collapsed against him, whimpering.

"Do you want to talk about it?"

She shook her head against his shoulder.

He squeezed her a little tighter and slid his fingers through her long hair, trying to untangle the knots that formed during her fitful sleep.

"Nate, is there anything I can do to help?"

Hailey's voice.

He flipped his attention toward her. "Just wait in the other room."

The words came harsher than was warranted, but he'd been specific in his instructions and didn't appreciate the intrusion in his daughter's sanctuary.

Hailey might get a lot of leeway from him, might always hold a special place in his heart no matter how hard he fought it, but she didn't supersede the needs of his daughter.

No how. No way.

Lori folded her shoulders, no doubt trying to melt into his chest, to disappear from the prying eyes of the stranger. He tried to reassure her but had to reach for the words. "It's okay, she's a friend of mine."

She leaned back enough that he could see her hands. *I've never seen her before.*

"It's been a long time since I've seen her too. She doesn't live around here anymore. Only in town to see her dad because it's Christmas."

If you don't see her, how is she a friend?

"We knew each other when we were in school together."

Is she nice?

Nate slid a finger down her nose, debating the question even though he had a clear answer. "Yes. She is."

After the words had slipped through his mouth, he

wondered if Hailey was still in the doorway to hear them. A quick check over his shoulder confirmed she'd done as he asked this time.

He lifted Lori's chin and looked down into his daughter's tear streaked face. "What are you afraid of, baby?"

Scary dream.

He kissed her forehead and pushed her hair back over her shoulder. "You know I won't let anything bad happen to you. Don't you?"

She nodded her head and then collapsed back into him, hugging his neck.

"Do you want a drink of water?"

She nodded again.

Nate found his feet and picked her up off the bed, balancing her on his hip. She tightened her grip and laid her head against his shoulders.

He paused in the hall, leaning back against the wall, trying to collect his emotions. Of all the trials he'd endured, nothing—not even what Hailey had done to him—hurt as bad as seeing Lori in pain or watching her struggle with the simplest things. If possible, he'd take every hurt for her.

His resolve cemented in his gut. Anything he'd felt for Hailey way back when couldn't influence this moment.

He felt bad for the difficult situation Hailey was in, but Lori's needs came first. Without question.

If only he could help Hailey see the truth about Bill.

The living room was empty.

He should have known she'd run again. Then, the smell of sweet chocolate hit his senses. He rounded the corner and found Hailey at his stove. "What are you doing?"

Hailey turned to face him. Taking a dishtowel from where it hung on the handle of the oven door, she wiped her hands, stumbling for something to say. "I hope you don't mind. I thought that maybe your daughter would like some cocoa. My mom used to make it for me after I had a nightmare."

Nate tightened his hold on Lori and took two long strides toward the table. Pulling out a chair, he set her down. "I usually don't let her have sweets this late at night."

Wedging his way between Hailey and the stove, he took the pan from the burner and turned the flame off. The kindness of her actions doused the acidic flames burning his stomach, but he didn't want that. Even though he told Lori that Hailey was nice, remembering just how kind she could be made it harder to fight for what he wanted.

Looking back over his shoulder, he asked, "Would you like some?"

Lori folded her shoulders, trying to make herself look smaller in the chair and signed a simple *yes*.

"She'd like that. Thanks."

"How about her daddy? Is he allowed?"

It did smell delicious, and he couldn't remember the last time he'd had a cup that wasn't made from one of those envelopes of instant powder. He was actually flabbergasted that she'd found baking chocolate in his cupboard. "Sure."

Hailey went about pouring her concoction into the cups and sprinkling tiny marshmallows on top. *Again, where did that come from?* His sister must have a sugar stash he knew nothing about.

He turned back to the table and grinned at Lori. Pulling out the chair she was sitting in he lifted her in the air. After he took the seat, he brought her back down to his lap.

Her giggle—music to his ears—reminded him of the light in his life. Confirmed what was important.

Hailey set the cocoa on the table and then dropped to the chair next to him and Lori. She sipped slowly from the cup, seemingly enjoying the aroma as well as the taste. As she set it back down, her tongue flicked across her lips catching every drop of the drink.

Nate tried to break his obsession with kissing her and gently blew over the rim, before taking a small sip. He hated to admit it, but it was perfect: rich, creamy, and sweet. It warmed a trail all the way to his stomach.

Lori slurped loudly from the cup, then set it down and signed to her father. *It's very good. Tastes like candy!*

"It is." Nate said. "Do you have something to say to Hailey?"

Lori hesitantly turned back. *Thank you.*

Nate bit his lip. He'd hoped Lori would choose to speak. "She says thank you. And I do too. This was very thoughtful."

She shrugged, but spoke to Lori. "Nightmares stink." Her gaze flickered to him. "I'm sorry. I wish I knew sign language."

He pulled Lori's hair over her shoulder as she sipped from the cup again. "She can hear. You just get shy around new people, huh?"

Lori nodded.

Hailey turned her attention back to her cup. After taking another sip, she ran a finger around the rim, wiping away a stray drip before it could fall to the table. "Your dad tells me you like to ride horses."

"Y-y-yes." She said. "My aunt…takes me."

"Anna works out at Sunnydale," Nate explained. When Hailey looked as though she couldn't place the stable, he continued. "Betty Crawford started a hippotherapy program out at her place."

"I don't know what that is."

"Therapeutic horse riding."

Hailey turned back to Lori. "Mrs. Crawford taught me how to ride when I was in 4-H."

Lori's eyes lit up and she leaned over the table, slightly closer to Hailey. "You…ride…horses?"

Hailey scrunched up her face and shook her head. "Not anymore. But when I was younger—a little older than you—I did."

"I don't remember that," Nate said.

"I quit riding when I was about twelve I think. I had a growth spurt and got too big to ride the pony we had. I remember Mom and Dad talking about finding me a more suitable mount, but my interest was waning."

What happened to your pony? Lori returned to signing.

After Nate translated, Hailey answered. "I just asked my dad that same question last night. Polly is living out at my uncle's farm and his grandkids still ride her. I want to go visit her before I go home. Maybe, if it's okay with your dad, the two of you could come along."

Lori leaned back, stretching her neck so she could look up at Nate with big pleading eyes.

"We'll see. Okay?"

She nodded.

"I'll call my uncle and see when we can come out and then call your dad."

Nate narrowed his gaze. He didn't think Hailey was trying to give his daughter false hope, but also knew she wasn't going to be in town long and had a lot of family issues to deal with. The last thing he wanted was Lori to get excited and then be let down when time ran out for Hailey to fulfill her offer. "Everyone is really busy this time of year, though. So we'll just wait and see what happens."

Lori nodded again.

He kissed her forehead. "Do you think you can sleep now?"

Lori nodded, and turned back toward Hailey. After signing "thank you" again, she slid off Nate's lap and scampered toward the bedroom.

The emotions he'd firmly grabbed hold of in the hallway were beginning to fade in her presence and he gave himself a silent pep talk.

Be firm. Be strong.

The past is just that. Leave it be.

"I do appreciate you doing this for her. It was nice, but don't raise her hopes about going to see horses. She's really sensitive and her feelings get easily hurt."

"It wasn't a false promise. I plan to call my uncle tomorrow and see if it's okay."

"Why?"

She pushed her chair away from the table and took her mug to the sink. "Because she likes horses. And I thought she'd enjoy going over to their farm and seeing all the animals."

She turned on the water and looked in the cupboard beneath the sink.

That brought Nate to his feet. Having her in his kitchen doing dishes came just a little too close to his fantasies for comfort. He crossed and took the dish soap from her hand. "You don't need to do that."

"I'm not going to come in here, make a mess, and not clean it up."

"Too late," he exhaled the words, then immediately wanted to pull them back. "I'm sorry. I just don't understand why you came over here tonight. Why you're being nice to my daughter?"

She put her hands up and moved back toward the table, taking the same seat she had previously sat in. "I just wanted you to understand how I feel about the house. I was mad in the diner earlier today, but not at you. The idea of losing the house caused me to snap. It was just one too many things to lose."

"I can understand that." He dropped back down to the chair next to her. "But I've learned something over the last few years. A piece of property is a thing. Things are not what's important in life. I want it for Lori. So I can help her."

"I don't want to stand in the way of that, but it's more than a thing. It's my childhood."

"I don't want to move into your house because of the value."

"I don't care about the money."

"But Jake and your sister do. They need it to pay for your father's care. Before you say he doesn't need to go into the nursing home, I'm going to ask you to take off your big-city, rose-colored glasses and reexamine the situation."

"Could you do it? If it was your dad?" There were no

tears, but a deep sorrow resided in her eyes and slumped shoulders. She wasn't even trying to keep her emotions in check.

"I can't even imagine how hard it is for you, your brother, and your sister; but life is like that. The things we have to do aren't easy. Doesn't mean we get to look the other way and pretend it's not happening."

She took a deep breath and let it out slow. "Jake took me on the tour of Pioneer this afternoon. After that, I had a long talk with my father—offered him a half dozen other solutions. He's resolved himself to do what Jake wants. I'm still not one hundred percent sure it's the right answer for Dad, but I promised him and Jake I wouldn't fight it anymore."

"I see." He didn't know what else to say.

"And I felt really bad about the way I acted in the diner. I wanted to make sure you understood that it was okay with me that you and Lori move into the house. Then I got here and I saw you... and, well, it just doesn't matter. My brother will give you a call in a day or two so you guys can work out the details."

It was everything Nate wanted, so why was he having a hard time accepting that it was going to be that easy. "You say that you're giving in, but I don't feel like your heart is in it."

"I'm not happy about putting Dad in Pioneer. I'm not one hundred percent convinced it's come to that, but he says it's what he wants. So, I have to accept it. If anyone is going to live in my house, I want it to be you and your daughter."

"Thank you. Lori thanks you, too."

"You're so good with her. It's so evident you're a wonderful Dad."

He felt his cheeks warm and hoped his beard camouflaged the blush. "She makes it easy."

"It might be none of my business, but what happened to her mom? Did she die?"

"That's my second favorite rumor." To be honest,

Nate didn't like any of the town-chatter about his single-parent status, but not enough to correct any of them. Since Hailey was giving him this gift—and she'd be gone again in a few days—he felt like he could tell her. "She just didn't want anything to do with us."

"I'm sorry."

He shrugged. "It's okay. Mt. Pleasant might not be New York City but it's nothing like this town. It was a bit of a culture shock and I did some things I'm not proud of."

"It's called being a college student."

She hadn't been the first one to try to absolve him of his errors, but for some reason—from Hailey—the words were comforting. "When Lori's mom found out she was pregnant, she just wanted to end it." He paused, flipping his attention toward the small hall leading to the bedrooms. When he was going through it, the idea of an abortion infuriated him. Now, having his daughter, the memories filled him with disgust. "I told her that I would be a parent and she could continue on with her life."

"She doesn't see Lori?"

"Never has. Not once. Didn't even hold her after she gave birth. The last time I saw or heard a word from her was a few hours after the delivery. By that point, we were long broken-up."

"I think it's pretty amazing that you stepped up, but I'm not surprised."

He never knew how to respond to these kinds of statements. For him, there was no other choice. "She's my baby. It's not always easy, but the only choice we have is to stick together."

Looking into Hailey's eyes reminded him why he usually kept the details about Lori's mother to himself. He didn't want or need sympathy from anyone, least of all her. Trying to lighten the mood, he continued. "Don't feel sorry for me. I certainly don't. Lori is a shining light in my life."

"You're special. I always knew that."

How did they get here? She'd shown up on his doorstep yelling at him, and moved to backtracking on her vow to keep him off her family's property to complimenting him. The awkward silence seemed to make her uncomfortable too, because she stood.

"I should probably get going. Dad is home alone." She walked toward the door, picking up her coat.

Nate joined her in the front hall and struggled for what to say. "I know things got uncomfortable at the diner earlier today, but I'm glad you came out and cleared the air. I appreciate it."

She reached out, laying her hand on his forearm, looking up into his face. Without a word, she pushed up on her tiptoes and slid her hands up his chest and over his shoulders, moving slowly, giving him plenty of opportunity to put a stop to it.

Preventing her never entered his mind. Suddenly, he was catapulted back eight years to the beach and leaned in to her touch as he lowered his head. His eyes fluttered shut as he anticipated her move.

Finally, she pressed her lips to his.

She'd initiated the closeness, but Nate quickly took the lead. His arms came around her waist and he lifted her to him, deepening the kiss. When it came to a natural end, several seconds later, he mumbled against her lips. "Why did you do that?"

She pressed her forehead to his. "I just wanted to... had to... one more time."

Chapter Seven

Nate paced the length of the kitchen. Why did he let Hailey kiss him and then just walk out of his house? And his life? Again!

His hands clenched into fists. He resisted the urge to take his frustrations out on his innocent kitchen table.

Why am I asking myself stupid questions?

Typical Hailey. Stir the pot... and leave. He never should have let his walls down.

He picked his cell phone up off the table for the third time in ten minutes. Once again, he tossed it down to the table. He didn't have her number. Even if he did, what would he say? Don't leave? Stay with me and my daughter?

That would be disastrous. Lori would become attached, and Hailey would eventually exit.

His parents' move west already proved his daughter didn't handle upheaval well. There was no way he could expose her to another round of it.

But could he leave things like this with Hailey?

He could call Jake, but what would Nate say? "I just made a fool out of myself with your sister and I need to apologize... or explain... or something."

Nate could hear stones kicking up in the driveway a few seconds before a flash of headlights shone through the window. Hailey had come back to talk once today, maybe it was becoming a habit.

As the lights circled the house and seeped through the kitchen window, he realized it was his sister, pulling her car around to the back of the house. Disappointment pricked at him, but he was happy for the distraction and retrieved her dinner plate from the refrigerator, popping it into the microwave just as the door slammed. "How's the horse?"

Anna didn't answer. After shedding her boots and

coat, she made a straight line for the refrigerator and pulled out a bottle of Nate's beer. She looked at it long and hard before putting it back, closing the door, and leaning her forehead against the surface.

"What happened?"

"The horse didn't make it. Then I was fired."

"What? Why? Crawford can't blame you because a horse had colic. You weren't even there."

"But it was my responsibility to do a final check of all the horses before I left." Her voice cracked.

Nate felt bad for focusing on the job and not Anna's loss. He closed the distance, hugging his sister to him. "I'm sorry you lost the horse. I know you care for each and every one of those animals as if they're yours."

Anna's body trembled in his hug, and a stifled cry—quieted by his shirt—reached his ear.

"I know you did that check, because Lori told me all about doing it with you."

Anna stepped back, shaking her head. Trying to hold off the urge to completely break down, he suspected. "The vet suggested the horse was given grain without being cooled out. And then he rolled before Crawford discovered him. His bowel twisted. Totally preventable, if it had been caught before he rolled."

"So Betty is going to hold you responsible because she screwed up? That's not fair."

"No one screwed up. The horse was fine when I left, but I'm the stable manager. Ultimately, it was my responsibility."

"I'm so sorry. I know how much you loved that job."

Anna leaned against the counter and rubbed her forehead. "It's more than a job. Always has been." She took a deep breath, and let it out with a slow exhale. "I was afraid you were going to be mad at me."

"What? Why?"

"Lori is benefitting so much. But now, if I'm not working there, she won't be able to go to the farm without paying for the time."

True, Lori would be devastated, but he couldn't be mad at his sister. He knew she'd never intentionally hurt him or his daughter.

However, this turn of events increased the need to get Lori her own horse.

"I'm grateful for everything you've done to help her. You didn't do this on purpose. You didn't do anything wrong at all."

"What am I going to do now though? I have to work."

"You're very talented. You'll find another job."

"Doing what I love? In time, but not around here."

If Anna moved away to find a similar job to the one she'd just lost, it would destroy Lori. Every single one of her issues would most likely get worse. "I'll figure something out so you don't have to move."

"Like what? And don't even suggest working at the diner."

There she went shooting his first thought down before it could even be spoken. "It is an option. At least until you find something else."

"Not for me. Remember? Dad fired me. He told me I could never come back." Anna chuckled at the memory and Nate couldn't help but laugh too.

At sixteen, she'd worked in the restaurant bussing tables for three days and broke several plates and glasses before their father—who was usually good-natured—had lost his temper and sent her home.

Nate always suspected she'd done it on purpose so she could take the summer job she really wanted—cleaning stalls at Sunnydale Farm. She'd been working there ever since.

"Just don't do anything rash. Give me a chance to come up with a solution," Nate said.

Hailey had promised to back off and let him lease the house. He'd planned to get one horse for Lori. Maybe his sister could start her own riding program. Coming up with capital would be a problem but the alternative made a talk with the bank worth a try. He couldn't just let his sister move away without trying to do something.

"I'll give you a little leeway, but not too much. I can't afford to be out of work long."

Thinking better of getting anyone's hopes up until he worked out the details, Nate decided to keep the seedlings of his plan to himself—for now. "Just give me a week or two before you start looking for out-of-town options. Can you do that?"

She nodded her head. She was trying to keep a brave face, but Nate could see the utter hopelessness she felt.

"I'm going to bed," she said.

Anna was halfway down the hall when the landline phone rang, something that rarely happened since they'd both started carrying their own cell phones. Nate might have written it off as a solicitor if it wasn't well past nine o'clock.

Anna spun back on her heels. "Good news never comes this late."

Nate couldn't argue with that. He reached for the phone with trepidation, shocked to hear Hailey's panic-stricken voice sounding in his ear.

"My father fell while I was at your house. He couldn't get up and I couldn't get him off the floor either."

"Calm down. I'm on my way over."

"No. I called an ambulance. They're loading him right now. The paramedics think he broke a hip."

She had the situation under control. So then, why was she calling him? Unless… "Do you want me to meet you at the hospital?"

"Would you?"

"I'm on my way."

Chapter Eight

Hailey picked her coat up from the kitchen chair. Without thinking, she ran onto the ice-covered sidewalk.

The paramedic caught her as her legs began to slide out from under her. "Careful. Let's get you in the back of the ambulance. Your father is asking for you."

She climbed up and sat next to the other paramedic on the small metal ledge connected to the sidewall.

Her father called out her name.

She reached over and gripped his hand. "I'm right here. I'm so sorry. I shouldn't have left you alone."

"Get your momma for me. Where's your mom at?"

Hailey covered her mouth with her free hand and swallowed the tears blocking her throat. Even though there had been episodes and indicators over the last few days, she'd refused to believe her siblings when they said her father couldn't be alone. She had accused both of them—and Nate too—of exaggerating the magnitude of his disorientation.

She'd asked for an ultimate sign that her father was as bad as everyone had said and now had seen the worst with her own eyes.

He'd been screaming for his wife since she'd returned home and confused Hailey for her mother for a second time in two days. And when she first tried to help him, he had used abusive language and swung at her once.

"Can't you give him anything?"

"We have to be careful about what we administer. I'm betting they take him to surgery tonight. We don't want to do something that will prevent that."

"But he's in so much pain."

"I know. We'll be there in a few minutes and the doctor will do what he can."

She bent slightly at the waist, trying to get closer to her father. The ambulance swayed as it rounded the corner and she nearly lost her balance. Holding her father's hand, she chastised herself for leaving him alone to go investigate her unresolved feelings about the past.

Nate.

After kissing him, she'd fled the house in an embarrassed state of horror. Why did he have this effect on her? Maybe avoidance *was* her auto-response to the tough issues.

But it was more than that. She'd almost turned around to go back to Nate's twice, but resisted the urge. There was nothing cut and dried about the situation. Obviously there was still a physical attraction, but their worlds were wildly different and so much time had passed.

Even if Nate wanted a second attempt at a relationship—and she wasn't sure he did—they'd both endured so many changes, they had to be different people than they were back then.

Still, calling Nate for help was her first thought when she found her father.

Seeing him on the bathroom floor and not being able to help him struck a panic. Feeling helpless, she wanted Nate's strong arms around her again.

If only...

Several moments later, the ambulance came to a full stop. Hailey heard the doors to the cab slam. "I think we're at the hospital. The doctors are going to help you."

Her father's only response was to moan. At least he wasn't crying out, but Hailey now doubted that he was fully aware of his surroundings.

The back doors flung open. The paramedic nudged at her shoulder. "Go ahead and jump down so we can get him out."

She followed orders, and walked the few short steps to the hospital bay doors. Folding her arms in front of her chest, she waited. So focused on her father's care, she didn't realize Nate was there until his hand brushed her shoulder.

"How did you beat us here?" It was all she could think to say.

He shrugged his shoulders. "You called and I came."

Her first urge was to step closer, lean on him for emotional support, but even though they'd had a nice long talk at his place earlier, it still felt like there was a divide between them. She pushed her hands into her pockets in order to resist the urge to touch him. "I appreciate it."

"I'm so sorry. Your dad is a good man."

"Why didn't I listen to Jake? He told me not to leave him alone for too long."

"You didn't know something bad would happen."

She took a couple of steps toward the ambulance. "What did you say about my big-city, rose-colored glasses?"

"You staying home wouldn't necessarily have prevented the fall."

She knew Nate was right—it wasn't as if she'd been following her father into the bathroom—but it didn't lessen the shadow of guilt that darkened her already dim spirit. "But he wouldn't have been all alone and in pain for so long."

"You weren't at my place for more than an hour. He couldn't have been down that long."

She turned back toward Nate and really looked at him. He'd answered her plea for help, even though she'd turned and ran from him. More than once. "I'm not sure why I called you."

"I'm glad you did."

She wondered if that kiss she had wanted for so long had meant something to him. She was still trying to sort out her frayed emotions but knew that it felt more right than any other decision she'd made since her mother had passed away.

But it wasn't only her life that had changed.

Realizing he was alone, she asked, "Where is Lori?"

"Anna came home after you left. She could babysit."

Jake approached the two of them as the paramedics

brought her father out of the back of the ambulance.

"What happened?"

She crossed her arms and took a step away from him. Toward Nate. "I told you on the phone. He fell."

"You said you left him alone. For how long?"

"I went to talk to Nate, about the house," Hailey said.

Nate continued where she stopped. "She was at my place an hour at the most."

Jake scrapped his hand across his chin. "Obviously it was too long."

"Just what I need, more guilt. I'm sorry. You were right. Is that what you want to hear?"

"I don't want to be right. I just want you to understand how serious this is. I want you to realize Kelly and I haven't been overreacting."

Hailey now knew she was the one who'd been misreading the situation. She'd been in denial over her father because it was hard enough to lose one parent. She didn't want to think about the other one slipping away. "I see that now. He's asking for mom."

Before Jake could respond, a nurse with a familiar face that Hailey couldn't put a name to approached them. Thankfully, she started talking to Jake, and let Hailey hide behind her veil of embarrassment and remorse. She turned, taking a few steps away from them.

Within seconds, strong hands came to rest on her shoulders. She didn't have to turn to know it was Nate. The way he gripped her might have given it away, or the combined scents of strong soap and the aftershave that had been making her light-headed at his house, but it was something more than that.

"Your brother is just angry and frustrated with the situation."

"I don't deserve your kindness. Not after everything that's happened between us."

"You apologized. We're moving forward. Right?" He put a gentle pressure on her shoulders, guiding her to face him.

She did without fighting.

"Right now isn't the time, but you're not leaving town until we talk about what happened earlier tonight."

In a moment of weakness, she'd given in to her desires and expressed the yearnings that still burned inside her. He didn't seem angry about it—he wasn't showing any emotion at all—but he was making it clear there were not going to be any more loose ends.

He'd drawn a line in the sand and insisted upon resolution.

If only she could figure out what resolution her heart really wanted.

****

Hailey and Jake followed the nurse back into the pre-op area. They'd been told the doctor would give them a brief update before taking their father to surgery. She'd asked Nate to come along, but he opted out, whispering in her ear that there wasn't a place for him in the family discussion.

The doctor stood near a nurses' station, all of the beds in the room were empty.

"Where's my dad?" Hailey asked.

"They've already taken him down to surgery." The doctor barely looked up from their father's chart as they approached. "It's going to take about two hours for me to get the hip set. With the anesthesia and the follow-up pain medications, you shouldn't expect to see him again until morning. My best estimate for recovery time is a few days here in the hospital, and then another ten days to two weeks in a rehab facility. After that he's going to require around-the-clock care for quite some time."

Jake spoke before Hailey could. "He won't be going home. He was set to go to Pioneer next week. Can he transition from rehab to there?"

The doctor nodded. "Looking at his medical records, I think that's a very wise choice."

Hailey closed her eyes and took one step away. "I feel so guilty. Is there anything I can personally do to help him recover?" Hailey said.

Jake spoke through clenched teeth. "Please. Don't reopen this. These decisions have been made."

"I know he can't come home, but does that mean I can't help with his recovery at all?"

The doctor turned his focus to Hailey, despite Jake's vocal dissention. "Often, traumatic injuries—like he's suffered tonight—lead to an even more rapid decline in general health. But, you can still play an active role in his recovery if you want. Most of the therapists here at the hospital don't mind family members being part of the process by helping with the exercises and being encouraging."

Hailey nodded her response. She could do what he suggested, and knew that taking an active role would be a good way to deal with her mounting guilt about being absent.

After the doctor left the two of them alone in the empty pre-op room. Hailey felt as if Jake was staring clear through her, looking into her conflicted heart. She started to turn and retreat to the waiting room, but his voice called her back.

"There's something going on with you." It wasn't a question. His voice was softer, resembling that of the big brother she remembered of their youth, when he was her protector.

"I just hate this."

"We all do. But I get a feeling it's more than that. You've been moody. Withdrawn."

"I've been really homesick for a while now. I feel like Dad needs me. Maybe I should move home and help you and Kelly take care of him."

"You said that last night. But what about your job?"

Hailey rubbed her temples as she moved toward a chair next to one of the beds. She dropped to the seat and struggled with the voice in her gut saying it was time to come clean with her family. No matter how she tried, she couldn't find the strength or the words to say that she'd failed.

Quickly, she ran the numbers in her head. There was enough money in her savings account to cover six weeks' worth of bills. She could go back to the city and continue her job search second-guessing if that's where she belonged, or she could stay in town, help with her father's care, and explore those feelings about Nate that refused to diminish. If she stayed, she could search for a job via the phone and internet.

"I don't have a job."

By the look on Jake's face, she'd just said the last thing he ever expected.

"I got fired just before Thanksgiving. I've been trying to find something else."

"Why didn't you tell us?"

"I didn't want anyone to think I failed. I figured I would find another job and then I could tell you all about what happened."

"Why did they fire you?"

"Because they wanted me to drop a case that wouldn't have a huge payoff. They didn't care that my client deserved to be heard. I wanted to go into law to help people, but oftentimes the final decision on what cases we took and what we let go were determined by the prospective payoff."

"If you weren't happy, why did you lead us to believe you were?"

"Don't get me wrong. I was happy for a while. College and law school challenged me. The neighborhood I live in is wonderful, all these little hide-a-way shops the likes of which you'd never find around here. I always missed home though, and over time, I've become disillusioned with what I'm doing."

Her brother crossed to stand in front of her. "I think it's normal to feel nostalgic, maybe even a little homesick, around the holidays. We've had a rough year with Mom— and now Dad—but you've worked too hard to give up on your career over a rough patch."

Those words of praise eased the sharp pain that had been cutting through her stomach for months now. "You don't think I should move home?"

"I don't think you're in a good place to make such a big decision. I think you need to put some time and distance between this pain and your choices."

"I don't want to give up on my career. I like what I do. But, I can job hunt from here while I help with Dad's care."

"How does Nate Jenkins fit into all of this?"

The complete honesty with her brother had lifted a huge weight and she wanted to continue the transparency, but she just wasn't sure how to answer that question. She shrugged.

"Did you call him when you found Dad?"

Hailey nodded.

"Why?"

"We were good friends once. I'd just left his house." Both were accurate statements, but they only scratched the surface of what she was feeling.

"I don't think you realize everything he's been through since your high school days. I know that it was a long time ago, but you hurt him once. Don't repeat history. He's a good guy and doesn't need you stirring up past flames while you sort out your restlessness."

"Maybe I'll decide to stay here."

"Do you really think that's a possibility?"

She shook her head and walked by her brother toward the door before pausing and turning back. "It's an option, but no. I don't know for sure."

"All I'm saying is don't make things more complicated than they have to be."

When her brother approached her with open arms, she went to him.

"We're here for you. Okay? We're family. You can tell us what's going on with you. All of it. Not just the good stuff."

"Thanks," She hugged his neck a little tighter. "And I'll

think about what you've said."

Knowing their dad would be out of it the rest of the night, Jake decided to leave, but Hailey wanted to stay until her father was out of surgery.

It wasn't fair to ask Nate to do the same though and she went in search of him.

When she walked into the waiting room, Nate stood and approached, meeting her half way. "Is everything all right?"

She recounted the conversations with the doctor, censoring out the bit about coming clean with Jake about her unemployment. "I want to stay here until the surgery is over, but you should go on home. I know you have to work tomorrow and you have Lori there who needs you."

Nate reached out for her hand. When she gave it to him, he tugged slightly, pulling her closer, then bent over and whispered in her ear. "While we wait for your dad to come out of surgery, we can go have that talk."

Chapter Nine

Nate fished his wallet out of his back pocket and handed the woman at the register a five-dollar bill, despite Hailey's protests that she should be the one to buy the coffee.

It wasn't about being a gentleman or any macho baggage like that. Not only had Hailey been through a rough night, but it seemed she'd been drowning in a sea of guilt and regret for a lot longer than the last few days.

She slid into the chair and rested elbows on the table before cradling her head in her hands. Nate eased back and resisted pulling her close by pushing his hands into the front pockets of his jeans. Yes, she'd opened that door at his house, but as far as he knew, she was still headed back to New York at the end of the week.

Even if he was willing to risk his heart, roll the dice, and revisit the past for a few days, he didn't have room in his heart for anything casual or fleeting. Maybe he could weather having her briefly, but Lori didn't need any more temporary people in her life. His only choice was to put his daughter's needs above his own desires.

"Your dad's broken hip isn't your fault." True but so trite. Couldn't he come up with anything better to say than that?

"I'm so stupid." Hailey sat back and met his gaze.

He shook his head and pressed his fingertips into his hipbones, still resisting his urge to touch her.

"I was scared back then. I left because I was afraid that if I stayed in town one more minute, I'd give up everything I'd worked so damn hard for to be with you."

Emotions that seemed to have been knotted up inside her for years, spilled out on her tear-soaked words.

Nate swallowed hard. Her admission slashed at the

70

walls he'd built to compartmentalize his pain. As much as he wanted answers, he didn't realize she could open up those wounds in his heart with a few simple words. "I just want to leave the past back there. It was a long time ago."

"It doesn't feel that way when I look at you." She paused. Her voice dropped. Even though they were mostly alone in the room, it was obvious these words were for his ears only.

"When I kissed you tonight, it was as intense as it was back then."

"We're not kids anymore. You live seven hundred miles away." Yeah, he'd done the math. Several times.

"Are you saying that if I asked for a do-over, you'd turn me down?"

"We can't go back in time."

"I know now that Dad needs to go to Pioneer. I can't take care of him on my own, but I don't want to leave him when he needs his family. I'm going to stay in town and help him through his rehab. That would give us six weeks to explore these feelings between us. See if there is anything to salvage."

She had feelings too?

Nate let his eyes drift closed. Maybe she had a point. Nothing else he'd tried to do since high school had successfully put her out of his mind or heart, not even dating other women or raising his daughter.

But, so much time had passed. They didn't even know each other anymore.

Did they?

"There hasn't been anything between us for eight years except for one kiss tonight. Not even a conversation."

"I've tried to forget you. I just wasn't ever successful."

"I can't be a shelter in a storm, or someone you use to get over whatever crap you're going through." No longer able to resist, he reached across the table and took her hand. "I don't have the luxury of being carefree. As much as I would love to jump in headfirst without thinking and just see where it takes us, that's not fair to my daughter. I can't let her become attached to you. Sooner rather than later you're going back to New York. Right?"

"Unless I come up with another reason to stay."

Nate didn't miss the innuendo in her voice but believed it wasn't anything more than flirting. He needed to stay grounded in reality. "You're too good at what you do and have worked too hard to just walk away."

"Why do you think that?"

Sometimes he wondered if he held on to that thought because it softened the sting of rejection, but he couldn't say that. He wasn't ready to admit how much he'd longed for her. Instead, he shrugged his shoulders. "It's what your brother and sister always say."

"They don't know what's going on with me. Not really. After Mom died, I began to see how much I'd separated myself from everything that really mattered—the people I loved, my family. I began to realize how lonely I am."

Nate swallowed the lump forming in his throat. She was making a damn good argument for taking a chance and exploring their feelings, but the part of him that had been taught by Hailey and Lori's mom not to trust still hesitated. "Are you saying that you might move back here permanently?"

"Private practice is an option I'm toying with." She pressed her fingers against the bridge of her nose. "If I would have done it eighteen months ago, I would have had so much more time to spend with my mom in her final year."

"If you want to open your own business, then you should go for it. Don't let anything stand in the way of your dreams."

"That's what you used to say when we were in school."

He dropped his chin and rubbed the back of his neck. "I still believe that." It sort of surprised him he did. Had he been following the advice?

"What if another chance with you is part of that dream?"

He swallowed hard. Every fiber of his body wanted to

go for it, except for his bruised heart. It was reminding him how this story ended. It said that if he wasn't careful Hailey wouldn't only break his heart this time, but she'd destroy Lori too. "There isn't anything between us anymore."

"That kiss meant nothing to you?"

Why is she doing this to me now?

He started to shake his head no but stopped. He believed picking up where they left off was courting disaster, but that didn't mean he could lie. "I don't know if I've ever been so turned on by just one kiss," he whispered. "But—" He scrubbed his face with his hand, looking for the right word. "We did what we were supposed to do after high school. We went our separate ways and started living our own lives. Can you honestly say I've ever crossed your mind in all that time?"

Hailey reached across the small table and clasped his wrist. He'd been trying to protect his heart by keeping eye contact to a minimum, but her touch demanded it. He looked into the stormy blue pools.

"Only all the time."

She pounded on the slammed door of his heart until he had no choice but to open it up. "A do-over, huh?"

"I know we can't go back in time. But, I'm going to be here for a while and it seems like we've both had a hard time letting go of the past."

This was too much to hope for. People didn't separate at a road's fork, only to come back together somewhere down the line.

Did they?

He turned his hand in hers as he stood. Guiding her to her feet, he steered her closer to him, sliding a hand around her waist. "This is crazy. You know that, don't you?"

"I think a little crazy is just what I need."

He pulled Hailey in tighter, and she curled her body to his. He laid his cheek against the top of her head, let his body absorb the closeness of her, taking a minute to enjoy everything he'd always wanted. Even if by doing so, he was opening himself up for more heartache.

Chapter Ten

For the next two hours, their conversation wandered through the past eight years. Hailey talked about her apartment in the city, her favorite park nearby—and how it reminded her, if only in a small way—of the one in town.

Nate talked about how he handled the transition from working in the diner to running it. He shared stories of raising Lori, the challenges and the moments of pure joy and celebration.

They were still lingering over their coffee when the doctor found them to update Hailey on the surgery. On the promise that Bill would be sleeping for several hours, Nate convinced her to go home to do the same.

As he turned down the road that led to her house, he couldn't help but wonder how this night was going to end. Her fingers had been sliding up and down his arm for the entire ride, and about a mile earlier, she leaned her head against his shoulder. Still, they hadn't really discussed or defined how they were going to move forward.

Maybe because he wasn't responding to her gentle touch, Hailey decided to clarify those lines—or lack thereof. She unbuckled her seatbelt, pulled her knees up onto the cushion, and scooted closer to him. Her arm wrapped around his shoulder. She pressed her body tighter to his as her lips nibbled at the side of his neck.

The temperature in the truck seemed to rise; he tugged at the collar of his shirt for air. "Uhhh… you should have your seatbelt on."

Sliding her tongue against his chin, she moved closer to his ear, nibbling on his lobe. "Come inside with me."

He turned the truck into her driveway, and she had to brace her hand against the dash to keep from falling. After pushing the gearshift into park and turning the key to off, he swiveled toward her. "I thought you weren't going anywhere soon."

"I'm not."

"Then there's no rush."

"We've waited eight years for another night together. I don't want to waste a moment more."

She'd been chipping away at his walls since the moment she'd come into the diner that morning. Earlier, they'd both been reluctant, but the moment she had declared her intent in the cafeteria, she'd pushed forward and acted as if the last eight years had been simply a brief moment.

So what was he fighting?

Having his heart shattered again.

Hailey had creased it once, just like Lori's mom. The walls he built had given him time to heal, but, damn it all, he was lonely.

Just like Hailey professed to be.

Was it wrong for them to keep each other company? He just needed to remember that no matter how steamy it might get, she was leaving in six weeks—maybe sooner.

He reached up and gripped a piece of the silk blouse she wore, giving it a light tug. She got the message and moved even closer.

With his assistance, she moved to his lap, wedging herself between him and the steering wheel. She hovered over him for a moment, before lowering her mouth to his.

Her hair fell forward and he worked his fingers through the blonde tresses, accepting her affections. He returned the kiss with all the longing he'd struggled to suppress for so many years.

She looped her arms around his neck and pressed her knees tight to his hipbones. He slid his hands up her back as she pulled him tighter, kissed him deeper.

"This is crazy," he mumbled against her mouth. "What are we doing?"

"Trying again," she mumbled the words against his lips before reclaiming the lead, capturing his mouth with hers again. Lowering her bottom, she rested on his legs. Arching her spine, she let her head fall back, exposing her neck.

Accepting her invitation, he mouthed the supple flesh, dragging his tongue against her collarbone and thrilling at the low growl she uttered in response.

When her hands dipped under his long-sleeved t-shirt and climbed up his chest, the realization of exactly where they were headed hit him like a bucket of cold water.

It was one thing to see if the fire still burned between them. It was quite another to recreate the past.

He pressed against her shoulders. "Not here, not like we're teenagers."

Hailey moved back on her heels, looking into his eyes for a few moments before shifting off his lap to the seat next to him. "This isn't exactly like that night. It was July. A lot warmer."

Nate twisted so he was facing her. Reaching out, he let a hand graze her shoulder. "It meant something to me. I just think you should know that."

A soft smile tipped her lips upward. She leaned into his touch. "I'm sorry I hurt you."

"Stop apologizing. Okay? It's over. We don't have to talk about it anymore." He wrapped her up in his embrace, and her body softened, melting into his.

Tenderly, she kissed his neck. "Stay with me."

The painful memories of his past tried to chain him to the seat, urging him to refuse her offer. "I don't think I should."

"Why? We're not hurting anyone."

With one arm he tightened the hold around her waist, with the other hand he gently stroked her hair. "You're in pain. About a lot of things. I'll come inside and stay with you. I'll hold you like this for the rest of the night. But, as far as the rest of it goes, I need a little time."

If Hailey had an argument for that, she didn't make it. Instead, she slid out of the truck and waited for him to exit and meet on her side. She then offered him her hand and led him up to the door.

Inside, she hung up their coats on the hooks of the mudroom wall and led him to the living room. As they walked through the kitchen, she offered him something to drink, but he refused.

On the couch, she sat on the opposite corner he took, but when he opened his arms to her, she came to him with the same urgency she'd shown in the truck. She laid her head against his shoulder and wrapped her arms around his chest. Reaching for the afghan that lay across the back of the couch, he covered the both of them and let his eyes drift closed.

Chapter Eleven

Nate was startled awake by his cell phone vibrating against his hip and the sound of his alarm slowly growing louder.

Five o'clock in the morning.

Crap.

As he moved, Hailey stirred in his arms. He tightened his hold and kissed her forehead. "I have to go to work."

She burrowed herself tighter to him. "Can't you stay a little longer?"

Sleep hadn't been immediate for them, but they'd laid close in the darkness and whispered softly to each other between brief moments of slumber. He couldn't deny how nice it had felt to have the company, and more than once she'd thanked him for staying.

"I can't," he replied.

She sat up, wrapping the afghan tighter around her shoulders when he slipped out from under her. "Can I see you later?"

He leaned over her, sliding a hand under her chin and leaning in to kiss her sweet, soft lips. "Why don't you come by the diner after a bit and I'll make you breakfast?"

She nodded before laying back down on the couch. "I will. After I go to the hospital and check on my dad."

He smoothed the cover over her, kissed her cheek again, and then headed for the back door.

Nate was almost out of the room when her groggy voice hit his ear again.

"I'll call my uncle too. See if we can take Lori over to see the pony sometime."

"Sounds good," he said, but her offer twisted his stomach in knots as he walked out into the cutting winter air and toward his truck.

The harsh reality of dawn had him questioning the logic of his actions. It was one thing for him to risk his own heart, but involving Lori meant putting her emotions at risk too.

He lifted his foot off the brake and scrubbed his cheek with his hand as he continued backing out of the drive. A balance would have to be maintained between Lori and Hailey, until he knew for sure what was happening between the two of them.

He'd talk to Hailey and make sure they were careful around his daughter.

When he pulled into the alley behind the diner, he cursed. Both waitresses, his aunt, and his grill cook were waiting by the back door. He hated being unpunctual but knowing there would be questions about his tardiness bothered him more.

"You're late." The fry cook was a regular Sherlock Holmes.

"Nope. Can't be. I'm the boss." He punctuated the sentence with a wide grin.

"You look like you had a rough night?" Shirley, his most loyal waitress, commented.

"I didn't get much sleep."

"Lori?"

He gave a half-nod but didn't say a word. It wasn't really a lie. She'd had a nightmare before he left the house to answer Hailey's plea.

He turned away and rubbed the back of his neck, trying to wipe away a pang of guilt as he unlocked the door. What if she'd had another bad dream after he'd left?

When they were all in the storeroom, Nate pulled the heavy door closed. He was about to get started on the morning routine, but his path was blocked by his Aunt.

"I'm happy for you," she said.

Anna always accused the woman of having an uncanny sixth sense, but there was no way she could know that he'd spent the night with Hailey. "For?"

"You've been doing it all alone for too long—what?

It's been almost six months since you went out with Nancy Perkins. It's about time you put yourself back in the love game."

"What makes you think——?"

Wanda reached up and lifted the collar of his shirt. A swatch of pink lipstick resided on the light blue fabric. "You're wearing the same clothes you were yesterday."

He closed his eyes and leaned back against the door. "Do you think the others noticed?"

"Who cares if they did?"

"I care. The last thing I need is more rumors flying around town about me."

"If people have nothing better to worry about than what you did last night——"

"You know they don't. And I didn't do anything but sit with a friend who needed the company."

He knew all too well what it was like to be fodder for the rumor mill. This news would be burning up the gossip chains in no time flat, didn't matter if the tales were true or false.

"It's okay to fall in love again. That's a good thing."

Wasn't she listening? "But it's not that."

She gave him one of those smiles. Just like the ones she'd given him when he was no older than Lori and had been caught lying about stealing cookies from the jar.

A look that said she didn't believe him in the slightest, but she was going to let it pass. "Well, you don't pay me to sit here and gab. You pay me to make biscuits and the soup of the day."

Alone in the storeroom, Nate looked down at the collar of his shirt again. Cursing as he pulled it off, he remembered a box of t-shirts bearing the restaurant's name on the top of the far shelf. He'd had them made for the staff to wear on the float in last summer's Cheeseburger Festival parade.

Short sleeve didn't fit the winter weather, but it was better than advertising he and Hailey when he didn't even understand fully what that meant.

He retrieved one and slipped it on before embarking on his usual routine.

Nate unlocked the cash register and turned on the coffee makers and the lights in the dining room before opening the blinds. He then stepped out to the sidewalk in front of the diner—for privacy—and called his sister's number.

"Have you been at the hospital all night?" Through her grogginess he could still hear concern.

"Yeah...mostly." Not the exact truth, but he didn't have time or energy to explain the details right now. "How's Lori?"

"Sleeping."

"Any more nightmares?"

"No. She's going to be up before long and you know she's going to want to go to the barn."

Nate rubbed his temples. For a few moments he'd forgotten that his sister had lost her job. If Hailey was staying in town, that threw a wrench in his initial plan to help his sister grow her own riding program. "Bring her up here for breakfast so I can talk to her. I'll tell her what's going on."

"Will do."

The moment the clock ticked to six, a steady stream of regular customers began spilling into the restaurant. Even though he was exhausted, Nate welcomed the business and the distraction. That was until Jake Lambert strolled in, taking his usual seat at the end of the counter.

Jake hadn't said too much to Nate at the hospital with Hailey the night before, but he knew her brother had to have questions. Too bad Nate really didn't have any answers.

He flipped over a cup and began filling it with coffee.

Jake dropped the still folded newspaper next to his plate. "How's it going this morning?"

"Same as usual." Maybe the biggest lie he'd ever told. "How's your father doing?"

"He was still sleeping when I called the hospital, but

they said the surgery went well. They said you and Hailey stayed until he came out."

"She didn't want to leave until she knew the surgery was over."

"Then you took her home?"

Nate did not want the conversation to go in this direction. He pointed over his shoulder toward the kitchen. "You want the same as usual?"

Jake leaned across the counter, lowering his voice. "Did she tell you she's planning to stay for a few weeks? To help Dad with his rehab?"

"Yes. She did mention that." Writing Jake's usual order on a ticket, Nate kept his gaze down. He didn't want Jake to be able to read anything from his expression. He wasn't ready to say aloud they'd decided to try dating again.

"I feel so bad. I can't ask her to move out of the house so you can move in."

So *that's* what Jake was worried about: the lease. "I understand why she wants to stay."

"I do too, but I know how anxious you are to get you and Lori into your own place. Can you wait about six weeks? If you have to look for something else, I understand."

Another farm could potentially help his sister. "Do you know of another place with at least a few acres of property?"

Jake looked away and Nate could tell he was searching the recesses of his mind. "I can't think off the top of my head, but I'll keep my ears open. Honestly, though, I really want you to move into our old place. I know you'd take good care of it."

"Your place has everything I'm looking for too. I'll probably just wait this out and see what happens with Hailey. See if she decides to stay."

Jake fiddled with the edge of the newspaper. "My honest opinion? When we get Dad fully situated into Pioneer, she'll probably move back to the city. She's put a lot time and energy into becoming a lawyer, I don't see her giving up on that now."

"Who says she can only work in New York? People around here need lawyers too." Wait a minute. Why was he arguing that she might stay? His head knew Jake was right. It had told Nate repeatedly this little fling with Hailey was for the moment, to exorcise the ghosts of their past.

Jake set his attention fully on Nate. "I know. And you make a point. I think she's struggling to get through losing Mom and now all of this with Dad. She feels a little lost. Kelly and I do too. But they say time heals the pain, and I think once she deals with her hurt, things will fall back into place for her."

Was Nate a fool for hoping to get the six weeks she'd promised him? "I guess we'll just have to wait and see what happens."

Right after Nate delivered Jake his usual breakfast, the bell on the front door rang out. Lori and Anna came into the diner. He only had to look into his daughter's big brown eyes to see her innocence.

Guilt bubbled up. She trusted him to be there when she needed him. Last night, he'd let her down. The last thing he should be doing is putting her secure family at risk.

An overreaction? Maybe.

He was long overdue for some happiness—or as Hailey had described it, some company—but what had Lori done to deserve a distracted father?

He rounded the corner of the counter and smiled when she ran to him. He patted on the red, leather-covered bar stool next to Jake and she climbed up. "What do you want to eat this morning?" Nate asked.

Lori's eyes flitted around the dining room, before she looked up. She signed *pancakes* to him.

He kissed her forehead. "Pancakes it is."

Anna patted her niece's shoulder. "Why don't we sit in the booth over there, sweetie? Go on and wait for me."

Nate leaned through the window into the kitchen, "Two orders of pancakes." When he turned back, Anna was in his face.

"She's already asking about going to the barn. She's going to be devastated."

"I'll explain. Let me get her breakfast then we'll talk." Nate picked up a carton of milk out of the cooler and the coffee pot from the burner. "It'll be okay, Anna. We'll figure something out. I already have a plan." A scheme that had more than one obstacle to overcome.

Nate crossed to the table where his daughter sat. She took the carton of milk from his hand and opened it, sticking in a straw. "Can...Aunt Anna...take me to... the barn?"

He leaned in, kissing her forehead, "I don't think you're going to be able to go today, baby."

The bright smile faded. She turned her full attention to the table and her milk.

"When your breakfast is ready, I'm going to sit with you and explain."

Chapter Twelve

Hailey heard her name being called...by her cousin? She turned, shocked to see Rhonda standing in the doorway.

"What are you doing here?" Hailey left the chair next to her father's bed and went to Rhonda with open arms.

"Jake called me first thing this morning and told me about Uncle Bill's fall. I came here as soon as I got into town. I figured it's where I'd find you."

Now she felt bad. It hadn't even occurred to her to call any of the extended family.

Rhonda stepped out of the hug and crossed to her father's bedside, she took him in with a look reserved for a concerned parent.

"This is all my fault," Hailey said.

Rhonda sat in the chair Hailey had just vacated. "I'm sure that's not true."

"I didn't believe everyone who told me he was sicker than I thought. Then I left him alone. That's when he fell."

"Where could you possibly go late at night in this town? It's not like you're going to find a twenty-four hour deli."

"I went to see Nate Jenkins."

Rhonda focused her gaze, and twisted in the chair so she was facing Hailey. "I saw this coming the other night. Do you really think it's wise to go messing with that fire?"

"It's not like that." Though in a way it was. She detailed the events of the previous day. How she had blown up in the diner when she found out about Jake wanting to lease the house to Nate. How she later toured Pioneer and then went to apologize.

"And that's all you talked about? Your house?" Rhonda asked.

"We talked about our past too,"

"Honey, is a couple of dates really a past?" Her words rode a ragged exhale.

Hailey wrung her hands as she walked to the opposite side of her father's bed. "We've always had a lot of chemistry."

"Yeah…sometimes with chemistry you get big ol' explosions too. Did your talk at least give you closure?"

"It opened the possibility of a future."

"How's that going to work when you live in New York?"

"I'm thinking about moving back here to take care of Dad."

Rhonda searched her eyes. "Why?"

Hailey knew she could see clear through to her soul. "Dad needs me, and I need to be here, like I wasn't for Mom."

"Isn't everyone going to get suspicious when you don't have to go back to work?"

"I told Jake the truth."

Rhonda's breath hitched. When the shock settled in, she exhaled slowly, shaking her head. "I know it doesn't feel like it right now, but you will get another job."

"I became a lawyer to help people. People like Mrs. Otero who deserved justice, even if it didn't have a huge payout that lined the partners' pockets."

"That law firm is a business. They have to turn a profit." Rhonda's defense had been the exact same words her boss had used when he ordered her to get rid of the wrongful death case.

"Everyone deserves justice, even if they can't afford the price tag. That's the foundation of our legal system."

"Look, I'm not trying to be cold. Maybe that client did deserve your help, but—as someone who runs her own business—I also know the importance of the bottom line. You can't continue to operate in the red."

"You think my partners would end up in the red if I took on one case like my clients?"

"Just one? No. But where do you draw a line?"

Hailey crossed her arms, and let Rhonda's words sink in. She made a lot of sense, but that didn't mean Hailey had been wrong to stand her ground. "You're oversimplifying the situation."

"Am I?"

"Yes."

"So, what are you going to do? Come back here and play house with Nate?"

When Rhonda put it that way, it sounded like she was running away from real-life. Just like Nate had accused her of always doing. That wasn't accurate, though. Or was it? "The last time I was really happy, was when I was with him."

"You were with Nate for one night, a long time ago."

"Now is the perfect opportunity to try and see if maybe there's more there. We're just going to see where it goes. No long term plans."

"Until you get a job offer."

She shrugged. "I feel like I've applied to every law firm in the state of New York and had every door slammed in my face."

"You know that's an exaggeration."

She shrugged her shoulders and sat at her father's bedside. She smoothed out the blanket that was covering him. "I'm still waiting to hear from a handful of places."

"And if one of them calls and wants you to start right away? What would you do?"

"It would complicate things." It surprised her that her first instinct, when pushed, was to go back to New York. Was that just because it was habit?

"Would it? Really?"

"Yes." When forced to think about it, she knew the truth. "If I had a job waiting for me in New York, things wouldn't be so cut and dried."

"Don't play games with him. That's not fair."

"I'm not. If I had a job offer, it wouldn't change how I feel about it him. I'm just saying it would complicate things."

Chapter Thirteen

The bell above the door announced Hailey's presence. Nate looked up just in time to see her unwrap the dark brown scarf, letting it fall to her shoulders.

He was struck with how polished she looked: every hair in place, flawless makeup, and clothes that came from a designer rack instead of the local box store.

Quite an accomplishment given he knew they were both operating on just a few hours of sleep.

The leather computer bag that was slung over her shoulder completed the urban professional look. It didn't matter that she'd grown up here. Time and distance had changed her. She looked more like an outsider than a local.

When their eyes met, she smiled and approached.

He met her half way. "I expected you'd take longer at the hospital."

She leaned in close to whisper low but still maintained a little distance. "I'm happy to see you too, sweetie."

Her use of a pet name melted his heart. He wanted to pull her in, kiss her cheek—at least—but didn't. Not when the eyes of everyone in the restaurant were on the two of them. "Of course, I'm happy to see you. I only meant..."

"Dad was still asleep. I talked to his doctor, and my cousin Rhonda came by to visit. I thought I'd let him sleep a little longer and take you up on your offer to make me breakfast."

"You just missed your brother. He said he was heading up to the hospital."

"Well then, if Dad wakes up he'll have company while I eat."

"Why don't you have a seat at the counter? I was just making the rounds with the coffee pot."

Her eyes flashed to the booth. "Is there a reason why I

can't sit with your sister and your daughter?"

Was there? Yes, because he was about to shatter Lori's heart into a million pieces. He touched Hailey's arm, guiding her out of the center walkway. "I need to talk to Lori. I didn't get a chance to mention it last night, but Anna lost her job at the farm. Lori isn't going to be able to take part in the therapy program anymore."

"Why?"

"Because I can't afford it." It was a simple truth, but the way Anna's firing complicated everything weighed on him. Lori had needs and he wasn't meeting them. Even if it was through no fault of his own, it still felt like failure.

The way Hailey dressed, he doubted she could understand what it meant to have to count pennies.

"She's not going to take it well," Nate said.

She patted his shoulder. "It's a daddy-daughter moment. I get it. Is it okay if I take a table though?" She patted the laptop bag hanging from her shoulder. "I've got some email to answer."

"Of course. I'll be over to take your order in a few minutes."

"I know what I want." Her focused gaze got the meaning behind her words across. Funny, he didn't mind feeling like a big stack of hot, buttered pancakes, when she was the one eyeing him.

"You do?"

She laughed. "Yeah, I'll take a house special, no rush."

Nate approached the large round table first, refilling the farmers' association wives' cups, making light, yet personal conversation with each one. His gaze kept flipping back to Hailey, who had made herself at home in the booth adjacent to his sister and daughter. He watched her set up her computer and hook up a personal Wi-Fi connection, Jake's words from this morning nagging at him the whole time.

The day before he'd seen the same old headstrong Hailey he'd always known. Last night, she'd been the woman he fantasized about, even eight years later. Today, even though she'd greeted him warmly, she seemed entirely out of reach—like back in high school.

His waitress filled a coffee cup for Hailey, making polite conversation. To any other pair of eyes in the diner, it might look like Hailey had successfully crossed the bridge between now and then, fitting in as if she'd never left. So, why did Nate suddenly have his doubts?

The voice that warned him she would leave sooner rather than later was growing impossible to ignore.

After making the rounds to all the tables, he returned the carafe to the warming plate and picked up the two plates of pancakes from the ledge. "I'm going to need one more stack," he called through the window. On his way back to the table where his sister and daughter sat, he let the head waitress know Hailey's breakfast would be up soon. He then set the plates he carried in front of his family, slipping into the opposite side of the booth.

After taking a large bite of pancakes, Lori dropped her fork and began signing to Nate, asking him why she couldn't go ride.

Anna reached over, grabbing her hands. "Lori, honey, you need to talk."

She swallowed hard and then sipped from the carton of milk. "But Daddy... says not when... my... mouth is full."

Nate couldn't stop the chuckle, but the news he had to share quickly chased the light mood away. "You know your aunt had to go take care of a sick horse last night?"

Lori nodded. "And you... made me... stay home."

Nate squeezed her hand tight. "The horse was very sick, and Anna had to pay attention to the doctor. They did everything they could, but the horse didn't make it."

Lori's eyes glossed over with tears. Her head snapped to Anna. "Sonny died?"

Anna turned away, shielding her own sorrow. Slowly, she looked back to Lori. "It's very sad, isn't it? Everyone at the barn is very sad. My boss got mad at me about it."

"It's not... your fault. Sonny... was... fine."

"But it's my job to take care of them. Mrs. Crawford got very angry with me. She told me I couldn't work at the barn anymore. That's why you can't ride today."

Lori pushed her plate away and folded her arms on the table. Burying her head, she collapsed into sobs.

Anna leaned over her, hugging her. "I'm so sorry, sweetheart. I didn't want this to happen."

Nate clenched his jaw. Anna wasn't to blame for the horse's colic and it wasn't fair that his daughter had to suffer for something that wasn't her fault either. "Lori, I know you're upset. I want you to remember that you and your aunt are not to blame. Sometimes bad things just happen."

Neither looked up or acknowledged what he'd said. Feeling helpless, Nate tried to lift her spirits. "Give Daddy a little bit of time. I'm going to fix it so you can have your own horse to ride. I promise. I'm going to help Anna too. You'll see."

Lori looked up and nodded pushing the tears off her cheeks. "I know... I'm not... worried. I'm sad... about... Sonny."

Anna rubbed her back. "It's okay. We all are."

Feeling Hailey's presence even before she spoke, Nate looked up to see her by their table.

Her computer bag was back on her shoulder and her coat on. "I'm sorry. I really didn't mean to eavesdrop." She turned her full attention to Anna. "Nate said last night that you worked for Betty Crawford?"

"Yes."

"If you'll allow me to represent you I think I can get your job back."

Anna looked at her dumbfounded at first, then nodded emphatically. "Of course. Thank you."

Hailey turned to leave, but Nate grabbed her arm. "Wait!" He flipped his gaze to Anna. "Can you really afford a lawyer and a lawsuit?"

"Don't worry about cost," Hailey said. "I'm not going to charge you."

Nate's gaze shot back to her. "Are you sure?"

"Yes. But I need Anna's permission to pursue it."

Nate turned his attention to his sister. "Think about this? It might make things worse."

"She doesn't have a job," Hailey said. "How can I make the situation worse?"

Anna was quiet for a moment while she considered what was being offered. "Yes. I want to do it. It wasn't my fault, and Betty had no right to fire me."

Hailey's whole face lit up with a smile that Nate recognized all too well. She was a dog with a bone, and it thrilled her. "All right then, let me get to work. I'll call you after a while."

She briskly walked toward the door. Nate slid out of the booth and followed her, catching up to her on the sidewalk out front. He grabbed her arm, turning her back. "Why are you doing this?"

"Your sister's rights are being trampled on. They're not going to get away with hurting her and Lori."

He stepped closer and stroked her arm. "I feel like it's more than that."

She placed a hand against his chest. "I want to do this for you and your family because it broke my heart to hear your daughter crying. But really, fighting injustice is why I wanted to be a lawyer in the first place."

The wall that Nate hid his heart behind crumbled. This wasn't a promise to stay from Hailey, and seeing her now in full battle mode, he wasn't even one hundred percent sure he wanted to keep her from what she was meant to do. He did want to hold her—thank her—and not worry about what anyone in this town thought about it.

Nate stepped closer and slid a finger under her chin. As he leaned in, she pushed up on her toes to meet his kiss. "Thank you for caring enough to try."

He escorted Hailey to her car, held the door for her, and kissed her cheek before she slid in. Only after she'd driven away, did he turn back to the diner.

In the moment, it had been easy to show Hailey the

affection burning inside him. Now that every eye in his restaurant watched him come back in and cross to the table with his family, he wondered if his heart had made him a fool.

"Do you really think she can get me my job back?" Anna asked as he slid back into the booth.

"I know she'll do the best she can. Jake and Kelly both say she's a top-notch lawyer."

"And she's... your... friend." Lori said.

Nate nodded. "That's right. Remember? I told you last night that I used to go to school with her."

Lori took another bite of her pancakes, chewing them thoroughly.

"She used... to have... her own pony." *She said we can go visit it.*

"She told me earlier she's going to call her uncle today."

Lori picked up her fork and took another big bite of pancakes. Nate could see the wheels spinning in her head. "Do you have a question for me?"

She dropped her fork and signed. *You kissed her. Does that means she's your girlfriend?*

Nate took a deep breath, considering his next words carefully. This was just what he didn't want to happen. It was one thing to take chances with his own heart but Lori's didn't deserve any more heartbreak. "She's a good friend. I'm very happy that she's trying to help your aunt get her job back. If she can do that, you'll still be able to go ride horses."

I like that she's going to do that, too, Lori signed.

"But, she's only in town for a little while. She doesn't live around here anymore."

"Far away... like Gram... and Papa?"

"Not quite that far, but yes. Like that."

"They visit... She can... visit... sometimes?"

Nate rubbed the back of his neck. "Sure. She can visit."

A large smile brightened Lori's face. She seemed proud

to have figured out the dilemma. If only it was that easy.

She put another large forkful of pancakes into her mouth and then dropped her fork so she could talk with her hands. *She's nice.*

After Lori had finished eating, Nate said. "Why don't you run into the kitchen and say hi to Aunt Wanda? I know she'd like to see you."

Anna let her out of the booth and watched her scamper toward the kitchen. When she sat back down, she focused a serious stare in his direction. "I saw your sketch book on the table last night and flipped through your drawings."

With everything else that had happened, he'd forgotten all about the sketch of Hailey he'd started until his sister mentioned it. "Seeing her again has stirred up a lot of memories."

"Which ones? Because, I remember how devastated you were the last time she shattered your heart."

"We had a long talk last night. I have my eyes wide open this time around."

"It's not your eyes I'm worried about, Nate. If you have any faults at all, it's that you care too much. And it's not that I dislike Hailey, either. It's just like you were saying the other night, she's moved on to a life of her own. Do you really see her moving back here?"

"I'm trying not to think that far ahead. She's going to stay in town six weeks to help Bill through rehab."

"Just be careful. I don't want you to get hurt. You've been through more than your share of heartache."

Chapter Fourteen

Hailey pulled up to the large barn and killed the engine. Having been freshly plowed, large banks of snow bordered the long, winding drive, but the small parking area was relatively clear. For that she was thankful.

She twisted the review mirror toward her and checked her hair and makeup, despite the fact that she'd stopped by home to collect some research, change into more professional clothing—dress pants with a matching jacket over a silk blouse—and touch up her makeup. The reflection staring back was nearly glowing, almost unrecognizable. A purpose shined in her eyes reminding her of a roaring fire. Unlike the woman who had spent the last six weeks bemoaning the loss of her job—sinking deeper into a depression—Hailey was ready to do battle.

Deciding to leave her purse and computer in the car, she locked it before shoving the keys into her pockets and heading for the barn's main entrance.

A few horses had been out in one of the front pastures. Because of the placement of the barn and a snow fence on the west side of the property, there were only a couple inches of fluffy snow in the paddock. The horses seemed to enjoy playing in it.

Once inside, she noticed a good number of the animals were still in stalls.

The facility was new, and larger than Hailey had imagined it would be. Over the years, her siblings had talked about the Sunnydale Farms venture. She remembered Mrs. Crawford from her 4-H days. The woman had always been enthusiastic about teaching kids about horses and riding. It didn't surprise Hailey that her former instructor had opened the facility to help kids in need.

That was about the limit of her knowledge of hippotherapy until she'd studied up on the basic facts.

In the arena, Mrs. Crawford's son Ben kept hold of the lead line on a small horse. He led the animal in a wide circle, directing the rider on its back to stretch forward and touch its ears.

Once that task was completed, Ben directed his student to find his seat again, then twist back to touch a spot near the tail. It was only after Hailey watched for several moments, that she noticed a wheel chair sitting on a platform and the limited mobility in the rider's legs.

"Hailey Lambert? I thought that was you." A familiar voice called out from behind her.

Hailey turned and saw Mrs. Crawford approaching. The woman wore barn appropriate clothing—jeans and a large blue sweatshirt. She looked as Hailey remembered, just a little older around the eyes with hair that was only a touch grayer. "I wish I could say it was a social call."

The light in Mrs. Crawford's eyes dimmed. "It's not?"

Hailey swallowed hard. Looking into a familiar face made this task more difficult than she'd thought it would be. "I wanted to talk about what happened last night. With the horse?"

Mrs. Crawford took a step back, pushing a hand into her front jean's pocket. "The Albrecht's called you?"

"Anna Jenkins. The horse wasn't yours?"

"No." Mrs. Crawford started walking up the barn aisle, motioning for Hailey to follow. "A few of the horses are mine and then there are a few—like Sonny—that I lease. He was a good horse for the Albrecht's when the kids were coming up through 4-H, but they're grown now. He wasn't being ridden much. I have a need for sound, well-mannered horses. The ones that are bombproof are hard to come by but are just what I need for the kids' therapy sessions."

"I think what you're doing here is amazing. It's so wonderful to hear how it helps the kids."

"Not only kids, I have some adult riders who are benefiting too. The equestrian disciplines and contact with the animals have proven to help with both physical and emotional issues."

"Like with Lori Jenkins?"

Mrs. Crawford smiled wide. "Isn't she the most brilliant ray of sunshine you've ever seen? She's such a star in the program. Not only has her condition improved—she was barely speaking at all when Anna started bringing her out—but she's begun reaching out to help other kids in the barn." Mrs. Crawford's smile faded. She wiped her hand across her forehead. "I'm going to really miss her around here."

"Does it have to be this way?"

"What am I supposed to do? A healthy horse that didn't belong to me is dead."

"What happened is tragic but not necessarily uncommon. I'm not sure you can pinpoint it as being Anna's fault."

Crawford leaned back against a stall door. "As stable manager, she was ultimately responsible for every horse on this property."

"Some horses just colic, though. Neglect isn't always a cause."

"You're absolutely right, but you tell that to the Albrechts. First, we were dealing with a perfectly healthy horse, who has never had more than a mild case of colic before. Then, the vet suggested he was fed while still hot. I know Anna would never be reckless like that, but what if the Albrechts don't see it that way?"

"So you fired Anna to take the heat off yourself? You didn't even wait to see if they were angry?"

Mrs. Crawford folded her arms across her chest and leaned further back into the door. "Are you just curious, or working as Anna's lawyer?"

Even though she was only trying to get to the heart of the problem so she could propose a resolution that was best for all parties, Hailey had to be completely upfront. "I have been hired by Anna Jenkins. I don't think anyone wants to see this get messy. I was hoping we could work something out before it all gets out of hand."

"That's what I did. To preserve my program, I let Anna go."

"On what cause?"

"Cause? This is a farm. I bring people in and let people go because it's the right decision in the moment."

"You can't do that. You can't fire her without a justifiable reason. I'll argue the colic wasn't her fault. You'll have a hard time proving it was."

Hailey could easily read Mrs. Crawford's body language as it went from defensive to outright angry. "Let me get this straight, Anna is going to sue me if I don't give her back her job?"

"We don't want it to come to that."

"But you'll do it if I don't cave? I can't afford to fight. It will bankrupt me. Why don't you go explain to Geoff and every other child in my program why you're taking their horses away?"

Hailey leaned back against the stall door and looked down toward the arena. She didn't want the farm—or the therapy program—dismantled. "That serves no one. Anna doesn't want that. Neither do I. But, she doesn't have many options. She likes working with the horses and the kids. From what I understand she's really good at it."

"She's very talented, wonderful with both the kids and the horses. I hate to lose her, but I'm afraid if I don't do something, the Albrechts will sue me for the value of Sonny. Either way, I can't win for losing, and the children are going to be the ones to pay."

"If I can talk to the Albrechts—get them to agree not to sue and say it's okay for Anna to continue working here—will you rehire her?"

Mrs. Crawford looked at her in silence for a long moment before slowly nodding. "If the Albrechts are fine with her continuing to work here and promise not to hold us liable, I'd be more than happy to have Anna back. Honestly, I wasn't sure how I was going to fill that hole anyway. However, if they do want Anna held responsible, will you convince her to drop the case?"

"Everything you've said is completely reasonable, but I have to take all of this back to Anna and discuss it with her before I can give a final stamp on any deal."

It was a better start than Hailey could have hoped for though, because half the battle was won. All that was left was to convince the Albrechts that Anna wasn't at fault for the loss of the horse. Then, everything could go back to the way it was.

"What about Lori? Can she continue with sessions at no cost as part of Anna's employment?"

"Of course, if you get the Albrechts to agree."

****

Sitting at the large oak table in the Albrechts' dining room, Hailey felt like she was intruding, even though she'd been greeted with a warm hug and then been regaled with one of Mrs. Albrecht's stories from the "good ol' 4-H days," as she had called them. The woman then insisted on putting on a pot of tea and scampered off telling Hailey to make herself comfortable.

Hailey didn't even have a chance to explain why she'd come by.

Mrs. Albrecht returned, carrying a tray with a pot of tea and two cups. She filled them both before sitting down herself. "How's your father doing? I was so sad to hear about his fall. That dear man has been through so much this year."

"He's doing better, but that's not why I'm here."

Mrs. Albrecht adjusted herself in the chair, folding her hands on her lap and smiling at Hailey, waiting for her to continue.

She quickly practiced the words in her head before speaking. "It was very tragic what happened at Sunnydale Farms. I'm so sorry for your loss."

The bright smile faded from the woman's face and she let out a labored exhale before dabbing at the corner of her eyes with her napkin. "We grow up on farms. We're raised to know that death is a part of life, but it doesn't make it any easier now."

"No, it doesn't."

"You know, I was invited out to Sunnydale just a few weeks ago, for the kids' Christmas party. They had a riding demonstration to show us what they're doing. Sonny looked so proud to be carrying that Jenkin's girl on his back."

"Lori?"

"Yes, that's her name."

"It's very sad that she isn't going to be able to continue in the program."

"Why is that? Is there not another horse for her to use?"

"No. Mrs. Crawford let Anna go because of what happened to your horse. Nate can't really afford to pay for the therapy riding. It was a benefit of Anna's employment."

"Anna Jenkins is wonderful with those children and the animals. Why would Betty fire her?"

"She believed you would want someone held accountable."

"Oh dear. I know I was a blithering idiot when she called last night with the news, but I don't think I blamed Betty or Anna. These things happen. Of course, I probably didn't say that last night. You have to understand, I was in such a state of shock."

"I can sympathize. You've owned Sonny for a long time, as long as I can remember."

"He was such a good boy, such a gentle soul, especially with the kids."

"I know Lori loved him very much, too."

The grief on Mrs. Albrecht's face morphed to concern, and she picked up the napkin from her lap, twisting it in her hand. "None of this is right. That child must continue riding."

"When I went out to talk to Mrs. Crawford this morning, she said that Anna could only have her job back if it was okay with you."

"Okay? I insist upon it. I wouldn't have it any other

way. Will you take that message to Betty and Anna for me?"

"Certainly. Thank you so much."

A wave of relief washed over Hailey. It had been much easier than she thought to straighten everything out, but—with the benefit of hindsight—she realized she should have expected this.

All parties were reasonable, but tragic situations had a way of causing people to throw logic out the window. People reacted in fear. Walls were built.

Like the ones Nate had erected between himself and her.

Not everything could be fixed by simply talking it out, but keeping things bottled up only made it worse.

Hailey hoped that by doing the work, and bridging the gaps between the involved parties, she'd shown Nate that she was committed to sticking around and seeing what the future held.

Chapter Fifteen

When Hailey had called the diner and asked Nate to bring up a dinner special for her father, he had hopes it would be the first step to an evening together, and was disappointed that Hailey had asked him to bring Anna and Lori along.

It seemed a little soon for her to have a progress report on her fight to get Anna's job back, but it was the only reason he could think of that she'd ask him to bring the family in tow.

He took two steps ahead, pushing open the large doors between wings, holding it for his sister and daughter, before following them to the room number Hailey had told him on the phone.

As they entered, Hailey looked up from her laptop. The smile she gave him said that she was as anxious to be in his arms as he was to hold her.

That little piece of his heart that was still struggling to keep things light and easy with her forced his gaze toward Bill.

"Hailey said you couldn't eat what they try to pass off as food here." Nate set the bag on the table and unpacked the Styrofoam container containing beef stew over biscuits.

Bill inhaled the aromas. "This is more like it."

Anna shifted her weight and crossed her arms. "I'm sorry to interrupt, but do you have any news for me?"

Hailey turned toward Nate's sister with a huge smile. "Mrs. Crawford wanted me to deliver this message, 'don't be late tomorrow.'"

Anna's jaw dropped. "Really? You got me my job back?"

A pressure lifted from Nate's chest. He still thought helping his sister get her own program off the ground was a good idea, but now they had time to build a plan without worrying about her making enough money to live.

Lori's face lit up. Tugging on Anna's pant leg, Lori began signing as fast as she could move her hands, as soon as Anna looked in her direction.

Nate leaned over Lori grabbing each of her wrists. "Baby, it might be best to let your aunt work for a day or two before we assume everything is back to normal."

Hailey bit her lower lip, looking as though she wasn't sure she should speak up, but then decided to anyway. "I asked Mrs. Crawford about Lori's riding. She says it's okay. But, I also talked to my uncle, and he said we can go see my old pony tomorrow."

Nate could see a longing in Hailey's eyes but felt his stomach churn. He didn't want to disappoint Lori, but he also wasn't sure that Lori and Hailey spending a lot of time together was a good idea. He looked down into his daughter's pleading face.

"Do you want to go ride at the barn with your Aunt or go see Hailey's horse?"

Lori stuck her lip out. *I want to do both.*

He turned to Hailey. "When did you want to go to your uncle's?"

"We left it open, but I thought late afternoon. That way I could spend the early part of the day up here with Dad. Kelly can come by and sit with Dad after her husband gets home from work."

Nate turned back to Lori. "If it's okay with Anna, you can go with her in the morning and I'll come pick you up after lunch so we can go with Hailey before dinner."

Lori flipped her gaze to Anna, who laughed at the young girl's hopeful expression. "It's fine." Anna then spoke to Hailey. "I can't thank you enough. Are you sure I can't pay you?"

"I'm absolutely positive. I didn't do all that much. Betty didn't really want to fire you, but she was afraid that the Albrechts would want someone held responsible."

Over the next several minutes, Hailey told the whole

story of her mediation between all the parties involved, impressing Nate.

When she'd first mentioned representing Anna, he'd been afraid that interjecting a lawyer into the situation would raise the tensions, but in the matter of a day, Hailey had turned around what seemed like a hopeless situation.

She'd found a peaceful resolution that satisfied everyone.

Jake was right. Hailey was good at what she did, and she would most likely return to it sooner rather than later.

How could he let her stay with him, knowing that she'd be wasting her talent?

Anna closed the distance, hugging Hailey's neck. "Thank you so much. It might be nothing to you, but the job means the world to me."

"I can't even tell you how happy I was to be able to help."

Nate squeezed Lori's shoulders. "Don't you have something to say to Hailey? She's the one who worked everything out."

Lori took a couple hesitant steps at first, then closed the distance between her and the chair Hailey still sat in. "Thank you."

"You're very welcome." Hailey looked up to Nate. "There's some other things I want to talk to you about. Can I come by your house in a couple of hours?"

"Sure. Let me go back by the diner and give closing instructions to the staff. Do you want to say eight o'clock or so?"

Hailey nodded and smiled at him. "That's perfect."

Nate hesitated a moment. His gaze darted between Hailey and Lori. It seemed so silly to hold on to the resolve to keep his morphing feelings about Hailey quiet around his daughter, especially after his display of affection earlier in the diner. Besides, he couldn't bring himself to leave until he said goodbye in the way that he wanted. Nate leaned over her chair and left a kiss on her cheek. "I'll see you after a while."

Chapter Sixteen

Standing under Nate's porch light, Hailey felt her confidence begin to waiver. Leaving everything she'd acquired in New York to come home felt like the right decision, especially when it came to the business choices. But, the piece of the puzzle that was Nate still felt a little disjointed.

There was no denying the chemistry between them, but she knew he was holding back, trying to figure out if she was someone he could trust.

To be honest, she was holding back too. She hadn't told him about her employment situation.

It was time to put all the cards on the table. Maybe if he knew there was nothing waiting for her in the city, he'd trust that she wasn't going to leave on a whim.

He opened the door and greeted her with a warm smile. After helping her out of her coat and hanging it on the coat tree, he wrapped an arm around her shoulder.

Wordlessly.

She let her body collapse into his. He tightened his clutch, holding her up as they walked into the living room.

He had the tree lights on and a fire in the fireplace in the otherwise dimly lit room. It was peaceful and felt like home.

Like her apartment never felt.

"Why would you ever want to move out of this house?" The words slipped from her mouth without a thought as she dropped down to the couch.

He picked up the bottle of wine that was sitting on the coffee table and began working on the corkscrew. "It's not my house." He didn't take his eyes from the wine bottle.

She felt like she'd touched a nerve. "I only meant that this is quiet. Where are Anna and Lori?"

"They went to see that Christmas movie at the theater in Bad Axe." He handed her a glass of wine and she eased back into the couch, taking a sip. "I figured you could use a little time to just relax. It's been a stressful couple of days for you."

Days? No, she'd been under pressure for weeks. "I need to talk to you about that. There's something I want to come clean about."

Nate's whole posture changed. Having filled a wine glass for himself, she'd expected him to settle in next to her, but instead, he leaned toward the corner, putting some distance between them.

He probably expected her to say she was leaving.

"There's a reason I felt so passionate about Anna's situation. I've been living through it. I lost my job in November."

He tipped his chin, looking at her curiously. After an uncomfortable silence he said, "I'm sorry. What happened?"

She waved her hands in front of her face. "I'll tell you all of the details later, but let me say what I need to first. By helping your sister today, I remembered why I wanted to go into law. Maybe it sounds childish and idealistic, but I really wanted to help people who have been wronged."

"That doesn't sound childish. It sounds like you."

"For a long while now I've felt like I made this huge mistake. I was disillusioned by law, thought it all boiled down to money. When I finally took on a case that I felt passionate about, my bosses told me if I didn't settle it or drop it, I would lose my job."

"And you didn't back down."

She laid her head on the back cushion and turned so she was looking at him. "This whole year has been about loss for me—my mom, my job, and now my dad. I didn't want to see it at first. Didn't want to accept that his mind was failing. It was the final straw to my own sanity."

He inched closer reaching his arm around her shoulder. "I'm sorry. I really am. But, I know one thing.

You're far too talented to be out of work long. You fixed everything for Anna in just a few hours, and did so in a way that made everyone happy."

"I need a new start. Or maybe it's an old start, I don't know. I'm moving home permanently. I already talked to the owner of that empty building on Main. I'm going to rent it and start a law practice here."

She didn't know what she expected Nate's reaction to be but the confusion that clouded his eyes wasn't it. He pulled up, twisted his body on the cushion. "That's huge! I don't know if you should make that big of a decision when you're so upset about your dad."

"For the first time in months, I know that I'm making the right choices. I only wish I'd had the courage to make them while my mother was still alive."

He grazed her shoulder with his fingertips. "But the type of work you'll get, and the amount of it, it's going to be drastically different."

She crossed her arms in front of her chest and pulled her knees up, resting her heels on the couch cushion. "I feel like you don't want me to move back here."

His fingers traced down her jawline. "Are you kidding? It would be amazing to really have you close, but it won't work if you aren't true to yourself. I'm not so sure this is where you belong. You might feel safe here, but is that the kind of person you are? Or are you the person who kicks in doors and shakes things up?"

She moved closer to him and he guided her to straddle his lap. She leaned in kissing his lips softly. "I'm tired of running away. I want to come home. To you. Am I too late to try?"

He gripped her hips, pulled her closer. "No. You're not."

She rested her forehead on his, "And I want you to know that until we sort this all out between us, you can keep a horse for Lori at the house. I don't want you to have to put that dream of hers on hold. The only thing I want to do first is check out the barn roof. My dad said it needs some repairs."

His hands encased his cheeks. "We don't have to worry about any of that right now. I want to give this some time, see where it goes."

She pulled back. "You still don't trust me."

"It's been a long time, eight years. There's no way to tell yet if there's enough here to build a long term relationship."

"I get that, but didn't you hear me? I'm not going anywhere."

"I can't get Lori's hopes up on anything I'm not sure about. I think getting her a horse and keeping it at your house would give her a sense that you're going to be a part of her life for a long time—"

"And you just don't think that will happen?"

"I don't know. Neither do you."

Hailey slid off Nate's lap, so that she was standing in front of him. "I don't want us to expect this to fail. I don't like being someone you can't trust."

"It's not about that. If it was just about me, I could jump in with blind hope, but it's not. Lori's welfare will always be a top priority. You need to know that going in."

"I do. And I wouldn't change that about you for anything. You're a wonderful father."

Nate stood, closed the distance between them, and took her hands in his. "There's no reason to rush this, especially if you're moving here. I don't want Lori unnecessarily hurt, but that's not about trusting you. It's about not knowing how we fit anymore."

She pressed her hips tight to his. "I think in time, we'll fit together pretty well."

He slid a finger under her chin. "How much time?"

Hailey pushed up on her tiptoes and nipped at his chin. "After last night, I decided to let you set the pace."

Nate leaned over her, sliding his mouth against her neck, then tickling her ear with his tongue. "I've been thinking about what you said last night about letting go and seeing where it takes us."

"Are you sure?" She captured his lips with her own, savored the taste of the wine still lingering on his lips.

"No, I'm not. But I think it's worth the risk." He kissed her again, this time tugging at the buttons of her blouse, pulling two of them open. "How about you? You said you want to see where this takes us. Ready to let go and jump?"

"I'm more than ready." She let her hands slide down the front of her blouse, pulling the fabric that was unbuttoned back together. "But you're not. You need to trust me first, and I can wait until you figure that out."

Chapter Seventeen

Nate pulled the truck up the long driveway, surprised not to see Hailey's car sitting near the house. He'd talked to her twice today and both times she'd confirmed she would meet him here at three p.m.

He swallowed the nervousness, and put the car into park. It was just three now. Any number of things could be holding her up.

Lori undid her seatbelt and knelt up on the seat. She leaned across Nate's lap and pointed toward the barn and the fenced in paddock. "Why not... k-k-keep horses... here?"

"Hailey told you the other night she doesn't ride anymore. Do you want to go see the barn?"

She quickly nodded, her hair falling into her eyes.

Before his door was even open, Lori had both feet on the ground and was running through snow toward the large building. Nate caught up and helped her push open the door, allowing Lori to run ahead of him. As Lori peeked inside an empty stall, he walked the length of the aisle, studying the line of the roof, trying to find the spot that Hailey mentioned needed to be fixed.

When he hit the gate, and turned back, he noticed the spot over the hayloft. Four boards were sagging in.

He grabbed a hold of one of the ladder rungs and hoisted himself up, climbing into the loft to take a closer look. The few sagging boards were beginning to rot, but the joist beneath them still seemed solid. He suspected a loose shingle or two and counted himself—and the Lamberts—lucky it wouldn't take much to fix it.

Hailey's voice sounded down the barn aisle. "I'm sorry I'm running late. The doctor came in to check on Dad just as I was getting ready to leave."

Nate came down the ladder and looked toward the door. Lori came from the empty stall and ran toward Hailey. "It's okay. We haven't been waiting long. I found the spot in the roof your dad is worried about. It won't take much to fix it. I can do it this week."

"Wonderful. He'll be so relieved to hear that. I just want to change my clothes and we can leave. It'll only take a few minutes. Do you want to come in the house?

"That's okay," Nate answered. "We'll wait out here." He checked his watch as he and Lori headed back to the truck. Her uncle's house wasn't that far away, but they were burning daylight. In another hour it would be dark.

Just as he got Lori fastened back into the truck and the engine flipped over, Hailey opened the passenger door and slid in next to Lori. He'd expected her to change out of her business wear into more barn appropriate clothing, but the only thing she'd exchanged was her dress shoes for a pair of snow boots and the suede coat for an old denim one that looked big enough to be her brother's. She dropped a canvas bag to the floorboard.

"Do you know where we're going?" She asked as she snapped the seat belt into place.

"Down one mile to Sturm and then south about a mile and a half?"

"You got it."

He hadn't even reached the end of the driveway before Lori was craning her neck trying to see what Hailey had in the bag. Finally, her curiosity got the better of her. "What do...you have...there?"

"Lori!" Nate chastised.

"It's okay." Hailey picked up the bag from the floor and opened it, letting Lori look inside.

"C-c-carrots!"

"As I recall, Polly could never get enough of them."

Lori and Hailey fell into an easy conversation—well as easy as Lori could. What surprised Nate was that Lori didn't retreat to sign language or try to hide behind him.

When Anna had told him she talked at the barn, he

didn't imagine it was like this. She still stammered, but she didn't let it stifle her train of thought.

When they pulled into her uncle's drive, Nate noticed the house lit up, but the barn looked quiet.

"My uncle said he'd bring the horses in and give them their grain, but I told him we'd give them their hay. Would you like to help me?"

"Yes!" Lori said. "I help...Aunt Anna...I know...how t-t-to do it."

"You can just pull up to the barn," She directed to Nate.

As soon as he put the truck into park, Hailey opened the door and Lori followed her out. They were inside the barn, before Nate was even out of the vehicle. He hung back and watched the two of them feed the pony carrots.

"They look hungry," Hailey said and climbed the ladder into the hayloft. She threw a bale over the side.

"H-h-how much...H-h-hailey?" Lori called out.

"Polly and the paint pony get three flakes each and that big bay gets four."

Lori began breaking up the bale, and Nate joined her. He carried the flakes as she separated them. They had given both ponies their hay by the time Hailey was down from the loft. She picked up two flakes, while Lori and Nate grabbed one each and they tossed them into the stall with the bay mare.

"How does their water look?" Hailey asked.

"G-g-good." Lori answered.

"Great." Hailey answered. "I'm really impressed. You know a lot about horses. Anna and Mrs. Crawford must be really good teachers."

"They are," Lori said.

Nate picked Lori up and rested her on his hip so that she could watch the pony over the stall door. With a little encouragement, Hailey was able to get Lori to explain to Nate what face marking—a blaze—Polly had. Lori also chattered to Hailey about how she helped some of the other kids groom horses before they rode.

"Would you like to brush Polly?" Hailey asked.

Lori nodded. "Do you...have b-b-brushes?"

"My uncle must have them here somewhere. Let's go look."

Hailey led Lori down the barn aisle and into a small tack room. On the shelf, they found a box with an assortment of grooming tools. Hailey picked up a soft brush, handing it to Lori. "How about this one?"

"T-t-this is a...good choice," Lori said.

Lori led Hailey and Nate back to the stall. Hailey put the pony's harness and lead line on, before bringing it out of the stall. She handed the cord to Nate, who looked a bit dumbfounded.

"It's okay," Hailey said. "She's not going to do anything. Just stand there and hold it."

He did as he was told and watched as the other two treated the pony to a thorough brushing. Afterward, they returned the pony to the stall and the brush to the tack room before turning off the lights and heading back toward the truck. As Hailey pulled the big door shut all on her own, Nate couldn't help but notice, the side of her he thought had faded away was still there. She didn't shy from the climbing in the loft or feeding the animals. She'd helped Lori brush the pony and his daughter had experienced a wonderful evening that she wouldn't soon forget.

"Daddy...I want my...own horse." Lori said after they had pulled away from the farm and turned out onto the dark, country road.

Nate exhaled a deep breath. "I'm working on it, sweetheart."

Lori yawned as she curled up against him. He wrapped an arm around his daughter's shoulder. "We have to get a house with enough land for it to graze and a barn for shelter," he continued to speak aloud.

"I'm hungry." Lori switched gears, as if his talking about feeding the horse had reminded her of her own empty belly.

Nate squeezed her shoulder. "I could eat too." He

flickered his gaze from the road to Hailey and back. "Would you like come back to my place for dinner. Lori and I can cook. Huh?"

Lori nodded.

"I'd like that, but," Hailey paused. He could tell something was heavy on her mind, but before he could ask her what it was, she continued. "We should stop by my place and pick up my car, then you won't have to worry about bringing me home later."

****

"Are you sure you don't want me to help clean up?" Hailey asked as Nate picked up the last of the dinner plates.

"I'm sure. Lori and I got this under control."

Lori nodded big. After tugging on Nate's pants to get his attention, she signed to him.

He paused and answered her in the same way and the child pushed one of the chairs from the table to the refrigerator. Stepping up on it, she opened the freezer and came back with a carton of ice cream.

"What about...Aunt Anna?" Lori asked.

Anna had come home when they were half way through dinner. She'd hastily made a plate and excused herself. Fleeing to her bedroom, Hailey imagined. She felt a little guilty that the woman felt the need to hide out in her own house, and was glad Lori had remembered her.

"Why don't you see if she'll join us for dessert?" Hailey asked Nate.

"I'll...do it." Lori said, running from the room.

When they were alone, Hailey laughed. "I get tired watching her. She's such a ball of energy!"

Nate's smile lit up his whole face. He brought a white box that had the diner logo on the top from the counter and set it on the table. When he lifted the lid, the smell of apples hit her senses even before he pulled out the pie. "She had a great time tonight. I appreciate you doing that for her."

"I enjoyed it too."

He began cutting the pie, and placing the pieces on

small dessert plates. "Is Dutch apple still your favorite?"

"How do you know that? I don't remember ever telling you."

He only dished three plates, before pushing the pie to the center of the table and adding a small scoop of the vanilla ice cream to each plate. "I remember everything about that date. The green tank top you wore with white jeans. You had your hair pulled back into a high ponytail with a ribbon that matched your shirt. I remember the way your flip-flops echoed in the empty diner as you walked across the tile floor."

Hailey's heart melted and she closed her eyes to the emotions bubbling up. "I had so much fun with you. Always did. Even when all of us kids just hung out together."

Lori came running back into the kitchen. She climbed up into the chair and pulled the unclaimed plate toward her. "She says...she's n-not...hungry."

Hailey took a bite of the pie. She closed her eyes and moaned. "This is so good. Do you do all the baking for the diner?"

Nate laughed as if she'd told a joke. "None at all. My Aunt Wanda makes the desserts and the soups. I could do the soups, but she enjoys it. It gives her a little spending money."

"Well, this is really good."

After holding her gaze for a moment more, Nate turned his attention to Lori, trying to include her in the discussion. "Everyone likes Aunt Wanda's pies, huh?"

Lori looked up and nodded. She dropped her spoon and signed to Nate. Her hands moved so fast, but Nate seemed to take every bit of it in.

As he spoke to Hailey, Nate signed and answer to Lori. "How was your dad doing today?"

Her gaze flickered between the two of them. Couldn't he see how exclusionary he was being? Hailey knew it was easier for Lori to communicate with the sign language and she didn't believe they were purposely keeping her out of the conversation, but it still hurt.

She tried to push the sting away and answered Nate's question. "Still in pain, of course. He doesn't like the therapy they started today."

Nate turned all of his focus to Hailey. "I'm sure that's more about the pain than anything else."

"I still feel very guilty over the whole thing. If I'd been home—"

"It might not have changed a single thing."

After Lori swallowed the last bite, she picked up her plate and silverware and took it to the sink, adding it to the pile of dinner dishes.

Nate looked at his watch and then twisted in the chair toward her. "It's getting late tonight. You can get a bath in the morning. Brush your teeth and get your pajamas on. I'll be there to tuck you in as soon as I'm done with the dishes."

She nodded to her dad and then stopped at Hailey's chair. "Thank you...for letting me...feed and b-b-brush your horse."

"You're welcome." Lori's footfalls could be heard as the girl headed to the bathroom, still at top speed. "Do those batteries ever give out?"

"Yep, usually about ninety seconds after her head hits the pillow."

Nate began running dishwater in the sink. Hailey stood and crossed to him, taking the dishcloth from his hand. "You cooked a wonderful meal. Let me do this while you put Lori to bed."

He hesitated. "Are you sure?"

"I'm positive."

As she did the dishes, Hailey tried to push away the feeling of exclusion that had come from Nate and Lori using the sign language. She reminded herself it had been a lovely evening with plenty of laughs. Nate had invited her to come to dinner and included her in all the activities.

And there was an easy way to fix this problem. All she had to do was commit to learning some sign language, at least a few basic words.

After putting the last dish away, she emptied the sinks and then headed into the family room, making herself comfortable on the couch.

A few minutes later, Nate joined her. Sliding up tight, he draped an arm over her shoulder and encouraged her to lay her head on his chest.

She slid her fingers up and down his denim-covered thigh. "Is she sleeping?"

Leaning in, he kissed her forehead. "Sure is. It took a little longer than normal tonight. She couldn't stop talking about going to your uncle's house."

"I'm glad she had fun." The conversation fell silent, and she held their entwined hands up. Encouraged by his touch, she brought up the subject that had been heavy on her mind through dessert. "I'd like to learn sign language. Can you maybe teach me, or recommend a good book?"

Nate twisted to look at her. She could see in his face he hadn't expected her to say that. "She can hear."

"I know that, but the two of you use it a lot. I feel like maybe it'd be easier for her to talk to me if I knew it too."

Nate scratched his chin for a moment. "I'm so touched by this. I don't know what to say. You're the first person outside of our immediate family who has wanted to learn." He paused again, took a deep breath and let out an exhale. "Of course I'll teach you, but Anna and her speech therapist have both been telling me to cut back on it. Anna says I use it to keep Lori close to me and separated from others. I did that with you tonight. Didn't I?"

"I know you didn't mean it," she responded quickly.

He lifted her chin so he could look in her eyes. "But, I hurt your feelings. I see that now. I'm sorry. I don't want to put barriers between you and her. It can't be like that."

"I agree. That's why I want to learn."

"We can do that. And I do have a couple of really great books I'll loan you."

After another pause, Nate pushed his shoulders against the back of the couch and stretched out his legs in front of him as he shoved his hand into the front pocket of his jeans. "I wanted to show you something." His fingers tightly wrapped around whatever he'd pulled from his pocket, but he hid it from her view. "Remember the other night when I said that you meant something to me, even back then?"

She'd never once doubted it. That intensity and need in his eyes back then had been part of what scared her. "Yes."

He set his fist on the thigh she'd been caressing and slowly opened his hand, showing a small hourglass style sand timer. "I made this my first semester at CMU. In my art class. I blew the glass. The sand is from the beach. Our beach."

She picked up the timer, inspecting it closer. The glass was delicate and detailed. She had to wonder how he'd kept it all this time without it breaking. "You were always so talented."

He took the timer back from her and flipped it over in his fingers, so the sand could run from the top to the bottom. "One minute. To represent that one beautiful moment that I held you close to me."

It was such a sentimental thought Hailey felt tears spring to her eyes. She'd been so reckless with his heart. No wonder he found it hard to let her completely in. "You really went to the beach and collected some sand?"

"From the spot where I had the truck parked." He set the delicate piece of glasswork back in her hand. "I've been holding on to that slice of time for a while. Now I want you to have it. To hold it."

She slid her fingers over the delicate ridges he'd constructed in the glass, admiring the details of his art. "It meant something to me too, you know."

"That's what made it so special."

"Leaving wasn't easy." She stopped herself. That wasn't exactly true. It had torn her apart, but she did it because it was easier than staying.

"You weren't ready. As much as it hurt, I wasn't either. I know that now. If we would have changed all our plans, we would have ended up resenting each other."

"Those dreams didn't make me happy. Had I stayed, I think you might have."

He fingered her hair, pulling her a little tighter. "I think you would have blamed me for holding you back. We needed to experience life away from high school. Away from here. We needed to reach for the stars, even if we missed."

"Maybe you're right. I know I've done a lot of growing up. I've also hit some bumps in the road. Even though you still have some doubts about me, I'm sure of what I want now."

"I don't have doubts about you anymore."

She twisted her body so she was facing him. "Really?"

He slid his fingers against her cheek. "The last few days I've gotten a chance to get to know you again. When you stepped up to help Anna, the way you handled Mrs. Crawford and Mrs. Albrecht, the way you've been with my daughter; you've shown me all those qualities I found so endearing back then. I believe you won't just take off. If we run into problems, I believe you'll at least try to work it out."

She leaned forward and kissed his cheek. "It means a lot to me that you feel like you can trust me."

He twisted to the corner of the couch, so he could guide Hailey to lie on top of him. He pushed his fingers through her hair. "It really touched me that you thought about stopping off to get your car—you were thinking about what I would want or what would be best for Lori—but I'd like you to stay. If you want."

"I want."

Chapter Eighteen

After spending the night at Nate's, the next couple of days became a blur. Hailey remained committed to spending time with her father and keeping tabs on his recovery. Her brother and sister split the time with her. As the week progressed, more of those bad moments showed themselves, fulfilling the doctor's warning that his dementia might be worsened by the trauma of his broken hip.

She treasured the good moments and did her best to help him through the bad ones but was increasingly glad to have Nate to talk to when things got rough.

He tried to resume a somewhat normal schedule at the diner, but each day he ended up taking at least a couple hours off after the lunch rush.

One day he spent that time at Hailey's side in the hospital, the other he picked up the needed supplies and fixed the soft spot in the barn's roof.

The evenings were divided between time for Lori and time for the two of them, but Nate also told Hailey he'd like it if the two of them spent a few hours alone.

When she asked if he had an idea how he wanted to spend the time, his answer had been skiing.

Downhill was familiar to her, but Nate was thinking cross-country. The last time she'd done that, was probably during a trip with her high school phys-ed class to the very same park they were at now.

Was Nate trying to gage if she was "too city" to play in the snow? "I haven't been in years, but it sounds like fun."

"Are you sure?"

"I am." At least she was sure she wanted to prove to Nate she wasn't the person everyone thought she'd become. That—at heart—the city had been where she lived, went to school, and then worked, but it hadn't changed the person inside, as they all seemed to think it had. That determination hadn't quieted the voice in her heart that was scared of making a fool of herself.

While Nate had gone into the park office to rent two sets of cross country equipment, she'd changed into the snow pants and down jacket of Anna's he'd brought for her, opting to keep her scarf, hat, and gloves. Though she picked up the second pair he'd thrown in the truck, pushing them into the pocket of her jacket, just in case.

In the first few minutes, she'd fallen twice. Each time, Nate was there offering her a hand back up. Quickly, she found her balance and was able to get the rhythm between her arms and legs working. Soon, they were traversing the nature paths at a good clip.

The scenery in the park was beautiful. The combination of setting and physical exertion was giving Hailey's mind a chance to process everything that had happened in the last six months. With each pull of her arm and slide of her foot, she exorcised some of the stress, negativity, and failure that had been polluting her mind.

It was a difficult activity to do and talk though. She was pleasantly surprised when they were about halfway through the two-mile trail that Nate slowed to a stop. A little way off the path was a bench—probably better used in the summer than the winter—but he led her to it and they took a seat.

"You thought you were going to trip me up with this, didn't you?"

He shook his head. "You showed me the other night at your uncle's barn just how athletic you still are."

Hailey giggled. "That's when you noticed I was athletic? In the barn?"

He leaned in close to her, grazing his lips with hers. "You've shown me on another occasion or two." He reached behind him, pulling the backpack off his shoulders and opening it. He lifted two coffee mugs out, handing one to her and then removed a thermos from the bag. "Are you cold?"

"You thought to bring coffee?"

"No. Hot chocolate. I was trying to duplicate your recipe, but I don't think I got it right. You'll have to teach it to me."

She sipped from the cup. It touched her that he'd tried to duplicate her mother's cocoa recipe, that he'd put so much thought into this date. "You're very close, just missing the secret ingredient."

"What is it?"

"If I tell you, you won't have any reason to keep me around."

He leaned over her again, leaving another chaste kiss on her lips. "Your cocoa is not the reason I keep you around."

She laid a gloved hand against his cheek. "It's not, huh?"

He shook his head, and then licked a dribble of chocolate from her lip. "No."

They sat on the bench a few moments longer, but the hot chocolate wasn't enough to fend off the chill. They both agreed they were a lot warmer when they were skiing.

For the second half of the trail, they moved at a little slower pace and were able to chat. Around the first curve they saw a few deer digging in the snow, probably looking for food.

They paused again and watched the animals until the deer became aware of them and ran off.

Then they started moving again. The first few moments in silence, but then Hailey found the courage to ask him more questions about their time apart.

"Did you ever get to play basketball at CMU?"

Nate seemed shocked. She couldn't blame him for that. Maybe it had been a mistake to darken what had been a light and lovely conversation with what was probably a painful topic.

But, he didn't shy away from it, and talked as they continued to maneuver through the snow. "I played two games."

"And then Lori?"

"Yes, well, in part. I twisted my knee and the doctor benched me for two weeks. During that time, I found out about the pregnancy and quit the team. I had to work to pay the medical expenses then provide for Lori."

"You paid for everything?"

"It was part of my deal with her mom. At least she let me stay in the apartment with her, even though we'd broken up. There's no way I could have afforded another place to live."

"You were good." Realizing the innuendo in her words, she felt a flush warm her cheeks. "At basketball, I mean."

"I did all right. It wasn't like I was going to go pro or anything."

This wasn't the first time he'd minimized one of her compliments. She didn't like seeing this broken side of Nate. It bothered her that she might have had a hand in making him think less of himself. She twisted the skis to one side, stopping for a moment.

He followed her lead.

"I stand by my words. You were a sharp player." She lowered her voice and peeked at him under hooded lids. "And, well, in those other areas, you're better than good."

His hand curled around his mouth as he tried to hide a blush. His other reached for hers.

Words seemed to escape him, but she didn't want a lull in the conversation. After they started moving down the trail again, she asked another question. "What about school? Do you ever think about trying to finish?"

"Sometimes, but not right now. Mom and Dad had to move out west for Dad's emphysema, so the restaurant is on my shoulders."

"That wasn't part of the plan either."

"No. But, that's okay. You know? Back then we looked into the future with these grandiose plans. Sitting here, looking back, I'll take what life gave me. Basketball and art were a very small price to pay for my daughter and the life I have now."

"You really mean that."

"You looked shocked."

She shook her head. It didn't surprise her. She could identify with what he was saying; it just took her a lot longer to realize it than it had him. "You were always smarter than I was."

He laughed. "No!"

"Yeah. I agree with you. The reality isn't anything like the dreams we had. That one night, I had everything I ever needed to be happy. It just took me a lot longer to realize it and find the road home."

"We'll see how it goes, huh?"

Something in his eyes told her he wanted this as much as she did, but he was still holding a piece of him back, wasn't completely ready to surrender. "Take your time, it's okay. I know I have to earn your trust, but I'm going to make you a promise. A few days from now, on New Year's Eve you're going to be the one I'm kissing at the stroke of midnight. And it is just going to be the first of many New Year's Eve's I spend in your arms."

He locked his gaze to her as they came out at the end of the trail, back in front of the park office.

She bent over and unclipped the skis from her boots. "Thank you, Nate. That was really wonderful."

Seemingly ignoring her promise for that New Year's Eve kiss, he picked up the equipment. "I'm glad you enjoyed it. Let me turn these in and we'll grab some lunch before I take you back to the hospital.

Chapter Nineteen

Nate rubbed the sleep from his eyes as he maneuvered the streets between his house and the diner. The late nights with Hailey and early mornings of work were beginning to take a toll on him. Like it or not, he was going to have to work in some time for a full night's sleep.

When he slowed down to make the left turn onto the main street, the engine began to cough and sputter. It was long overdue for maintenance and Nate wondered if it might be time to replace it. After all, he'd had the truck a decade now and it wasn't new when he bought it.

It struck him as funny. Now that Hailey was back, he felt like he could let go of the truck. He had to wonder if he'd held onto it all this time for the memories of the two of them?

Not that he wanted to liken himself to some of his classmates—the ones who had nothing better to do than sit up at the bar talking about their glory days a decade after the fact. His truck wasn't like a trophy. Yet, when he sat behind the wheel, he couldn't help but think of Hailey and that first night they'd spent together.

As he turned into the alley behind the diner, the phone rang and her number flashed on the screen. He picked it up and pressed the button. "Good morning,"

"Same to you, sweetie." Her voice was a little horse.

"What are you doing up this early?"

"I set my alarm. I wanted to call and say hi before you got to work."

Warmth spread through his chest. He could get used to this. Because of Lori, they'd ended each night—even if it was early in the morning—by returning to their own beds in their own houses, but for the last three days, she called to talk to him while he drove in. "Will I see you today?"

"Mmm-hmmm. After I get some more sleep, I'm going to head to the hospital and help Dad with his therapy. The doctor is talking about moving him to the rehab facility today. So, I need to talk all that over with Jake. How about if I come by after your lunch rush? About two o'clock?"

"Sounds good. If you need anything at the hospital, call me." Having parked the truck, he leaned his elbow against the window and his head against his hand. Through the windshield he could see his aunt and his fry cook waiting for him to unlock the doors. Wanda had a large smile on her face, seeing him on the phone.

"Hey... get some more sleep. I'll talk to you later." He flipped the phone off and got out of the truck. Pushing it into his back pocket and swinging his keys on the ring finger of his other hand, he walked toward the door and his waiting employees.

"Troubles at home?" Her voice had that all knowing lilt.

She knew he'd been talking to Hailey but was going to make him say it. "Nope. Everything is fine. Anna and Lori were both sleeping soundly when I left." Saying that, he realized it had been the first time in a long time that Lori hadn't woken up with nightmares.

"I see," she said as they walked into the storage room. "A little early to be making phone calls."

He couldn't contain the large smile. He could be just as coy as Wanda was. "I wasn't making them. I was receiving one. What's the soup of the day going to be?"

"Oh I was thinking of maybe doing something like Italian Wedding soup."

She was still referring to his phone call. That much was obvious. "Whoa-now. Way, *way* too soon."

****

As the lunch rush started to slow, Nate found his gaze flipping between his watch and the front door. Even though he knew Hailey's time prediction had been an estimate, he still found himself counting the minutes until he saw her again.

A half-hour later, she crossed the threshold. She smiled at him, but he could see that below the façade, she carried a lot of stress.

He filled two glasses with cola and let the waitress behind the counter know he was taking a break before joining Hailey in a booth. "How did everything go at the hospital?"

She took a sip from the glass. "Really good. Dad seems to be in less pain and he worked hard in the therapy session."

It wasn't her father's health that had her worried. Then what? "Are they moving him to the rehabilitation facility?"

"First thing tomorrow morning."

She answered his questions, but he could see the real story was in the unspoken words. After a moment, she reached into her purse and pulled out a folded piece of paper.

"I got an email this morning. From a law firm in the city."

He took the offered paper and unfolded it. Scanning the first paragraph, he realized that she'd been offered a job. Not just any job offer, a darn good one.

His shoulders dropped like a deflating balloon and a lump formed in his throat. At least this time she was talking to him before she left. "When do you have to go?"

She reached for the email. "I'm not. I just wanted to be honest and tell you about it."

"What do you mean you're not? This is a fantastic offer." Her annual salary would be more than the diner had netted in the last two years.

"I didn't even apply to this firm. The email was a total shock. I made a couple of phone calls, and it turns out Rhonda's father knows one of the managing partners. I never would have gotten this if my uncle hadn't called in a favor."

"That doesn't mean you let this kind of opportunity pass by."

"She's just trying to prove a point to me."

"There isn't anything wrong with accepting help from your family."

Hailey tossed the paper down to the table and leaned back in the booth crossing her arms in front of her chest. "Really? You want me to leave?"

Want this? Hell, no. But part of him had expected it. Even knew it was coming. So why was it ripping him in two. "I don't want you to give up a job offer like that. In time, you'll end up resenting me. Then you'll just leave anyway."

"You're wrong. I want *this*." She pointed back and forth between the two of them. "Whatever this is that I ran away from before, I want to stay and figure it out now. How many times do I have to say it before you believe me?"

How easy would it be to say okay and accept this time around she had chosen a chance at love over a great career? Fear pulled him back from the ledge, refused to let him blindly jump.

Rhonda and Jake had both warned her moving back home was just something she was going through: a crisis. Rhonda believed it so much she was trying to prove it to Hailey. Everyone in Hailey's life—but her—believed she belonged in the city. It wasn't fair to hold her tight. In time, she'd resist the restraints and flee from him.

And Lori.

Why hadn't he listened to his heart on this one? Backed off when she'd come at him—or at the very least kept Lori protected from the inevitable heartache.

"You need to explore this job. If you don't, you'll regret it. Not this week. Maybe not next. But someday."

"No. You're wrong. I did tell Rhonda the other day that a job offer might change things, but I know differently now."

Nate felt his throat tighten. While she was telling him she was here for the long haul, she was telling her cousin it was only until something better came along. "You said that?"

"As soon as I saw this email, I chose you and Lori. Without hesitation."

Nate dug his nails into his jeans beneath the table, searching for the strength to do what he knew needed to be done. "These last few days have been great, but we need to stop this."

"What are you doing? Putting me through some test?"

He shook his head. "You're not a small town girl anymore. You're definitely not a small town lawyer. This way of life is too distant from your apartment in the Village and Sax Fifth Avenue."

"Stop it. That's *not* who I am!"

He flattened out the crinkled page on the table in front of her and pointed to the line that included a salary offer. "Do you know how long it would take me to earn that much money?"

"What makes you think I ever planned on living off what you make? I told you I want to build my own practice here."

"That takes time."

"I know that."

He tapped his finger on the amount again. "This community would never give you this kind of income."

"It's not all about the money! Money won't bring my mom back. It won't repair my father's mind. I'll be damned if I let it come between you and me."

"That's easy to say now. But in time…"

"Let's talk about time. In eight years there wasn't a single day that passed without me thinking about you, without me thinking about that night in the back of your old pickup truck. I suspect it's been the same for you, or you would have gotten rid of it a long time ago."

She knew the same realization he'd come to this morning, but he couldn't say it. Brick by brick, the protective wall she'd busted through was erecting itself once again. "I kept the truck because I couldn't afford anything else. Nothing more."

"If I stay—"

"It won't work."

"Then why don't you and Lori come to the city with me?"

Nate felt his chest tighten. He just wasn't the kind of guy who could live day in and day out in one of the busiest cities of the world. "This is foolish. It doesn't matter. We're over. There isn't any room in Lori's and my life for you. We have to stop living in the past, wake up from this Christmas fantasy and get back to our real lives."

Hailey's eyes began to glaze over and Nate knew if he didn't leave right now, she would break his will. He'd admit he didn't mean a word of it and take her back in his arms, kiss her sweet lips.

But it would only be temporary.

Nate slid out of the booth and started for the kitchen. He didn't turn back when she called his name. Just murmured, "I'll be back later," to his head waitress before going through the kitchen and stock room. He grabbed his coat from the hook by the door and slipped it on, pulling the truck keys from the pocket.

He slammed the door, turned the key and started to throw it into reverse when he saw Hailey through the windshield coming from the back of the restaurant. She rounded the truck and tried to open the passenger door, but it was locked.

"Go back to New York!"

She slapped her hand against the window. "Open this door! Talk to me."

He closed his eyes tight, counting to five. He couldn't follow his own heart and let her in the truck and his life, not when he knew the best thing for her waited back in the city. "There's nothing left to talk about."

He started to back up. Slowly at first, but when she jumped away, he picked up his speed and pointed the truck for home.

****

Nate parked at the end of his drive and stepped out

into the snow bank. He slammed the door, flakes of rust dropped from the bottom, falling against the white snow. He stepped back as Hailey's accusatory words in the diner rolled through his mind.

He started for the house but then fished the keys out of his pocket.

Screw this. What was he thinking? Damn the truck and the memories it held. He wanted Hailey.

Two steps back toward the vehicle and he spun again.

No!

Forget what his heart wanted. His mind and his gut had been down this road with her before. A few days of fun was one thing, but he could never stand in the way of that job. It was laughable to think the restaurant would ever produce a similar income to the one she offered. She would never get the cases in the farming community that she would in New York.

Eventually she'd get bored. Bored with the slower lifestyle. Bored with him.

She was too good at what she did and too far gone from the small town way of life to be completely content here. He knew that way back then. It'd been proven again today.

Putting off the inevitable was the smart thing to do. As much as this hurt, it would be worse later.

Or had he taken a page out of her book and was running away from what scared him most?

Chapter Twenty

Hailey spent twenty minutes driving to different family member's houses before she found Rhonda's car sitting in front of her uncle's house. Neither one of them was leaving town before Rhonda heard exactly how Hailey felt about the interference in her life.

Her cousin opened the door and stepped aside, letting Hailey in to the entry. She nearly ran into a packed suitcase with Rhonda's coat laying over it. "So, were you going to mess up my life then run for home?"

Rhonda shrugged her shoulder. "I was hoping for a thank you. After all, my father got you in at a great law firm. They're willing to give you some lee-way on the kinds of cases you take to trial too."

"You cost me Nate! Even though I told him about the offer—made it clear I didn't want the job—he still broke up with me."

"I'm sorry. I know you don't want to hear this, but I think he's right. You don't belong here. This last year has been one crisis after the other for you. But tomorrow, we get to push a reset button. For you, a new year is going to be a new start and a new job. You'll see. You can bounce back from everything that's happened to you."

Hailey squared her shoulders and met Rhonda's stare. "Why is no one listening to me? I want that fresh start to be here with Nate."

Rhonda closed the distance, pulled her into a hug. "You know that's not moving forward. He's a symbol of a less complicated past."

Hailey pulled herself out of her cousin's embrace. "You don't know. I'm so tired of everyone around me telling me what I'm going through and what I'm feeling. I know what I want."

"You're not interested in that job at all?"

Hailey leaned back against the door. If she were to be completely honest, when she opened the email, her heart skipped a beat. The idea of being back in the big game thrilled her... for about thirty seconds. Then, she thought of the few days and nights with Nate and Lori. From taking Lori to the horses to skiing with Nate, from the family dinner to the quiet evening sharing some wine. She'd felt her life had come full circle—a happiness she hadn't felt in quite some time—and didn't want to give it up for a return to the city.

So, Nate had made that decision for her, protected his own heart and Lori's from what he assumed would be the inevitable.

To him, she was an open book, a transparent shell. He'd always known her heart, and believed when the going got tough, she ran. The piece of her that wanted to stay behind and prove him wrong submitted to part that was sick and tired of proving she'd changed.

"Okay."

"You're going to take the job?"

She nodded her head. "I'm going to go pack the car and go home. I'll meet with your dad's friend and talk about it."

Her cousin smiled. Not one of being proven right, but a smile that said she was truly happy. "Call me. Let me know how it goes?"

Hailey nodded and let herself out, wondering if this was the right answer why it was breaking her heart in two.

****

As Hailey came down the steps with her two suitcases, she heard her brother calling her name from the kitchen. She hollered out to him and they met up in the living room.

"Rhonda just called me," Jake said.

"So, you know I'm leaving."

He nodded once.

"I'm still committed to helping out with Dad. I will be back in about a week. "

"I realized the other day I haven't told you enough how proud I am of you. We all are."

She dropped the bags and threw her arms around her brother's neck. "You can go ahead and rent the house to Nate and Lori. I won't fight it. In fact, I like the idea of them being here." Her voice cracked and a lump formed in her throat.

Jake tightened the embrace. "It's going to be okay."

She collapsed against her big brother. "No. It's not. I don't want to go. I want to stay with Nate."

"Then stay."

"He doesn't want me. He told me to go take the job because we don't have a future anyway." She pulled back and wiped a tear off her cheek. "I think he's afraid of standing in the way of my future. He wouldn't listen to me when I told him he was more important than any job."

"Give him some time to cool off then go talk to him."

Hailey shook her head. "That was my initial thought, but—when it comes down to it—he doesn't trust me. He can't forgive me for leaving back then and has himself convinced I will eventually do it again. I'm not sure I can overcome that. Without trust, we didn't have a chance anyway."

Jake didn't respond, only nodded. "Are you sure you want to leave now? Would it be better to wait until morning?"

"I called the firm. They can meet with me tomorrow afternoon. I need to get at least part way there tonight in order to make the meeting. I'm going to stop by and say good bye to Dad and then get on the road."

Chapter Twenty-One

Nate shifted his weight in the chair, checking his watch again.

It'd been hours since he put a very abrupt end to his relationship with Hailey. Somehow it felt like days and weeks had passed. He hungered for another taste of her lips, and craved the touch of her flesh to his.

Part of him had expected her to show up, and once again push at his defensive walls until he crumbled and took her back in his arms.

A knock on the front door pulled him out of tangled thoughts. *There* she was. He thought about not answering but couldn't stop himself from standing and walking to the door, chanting the mantra to stay strong.

Pulling the dingy curtain aside, he saw Jake standing on the front steps, and reluctantly let him in. "What's up?"

"I went by the diner looking for you, buddy. You've taken a lot of time off this week."

"Well things will be getting back to normal starting tomorrow." Nate led Jake into the living room, reaching for the right words. "I ended things with Hailey."

"I know. I went by the house and talked to her for a few minutes before she left."

"She's gone?"

"I imagine. She was going to stop by the hospital to say good-bye to Dad, but she wanted to make it to Pennsylvania tonight. She's got a meeting tomorrow afternoon with the firm that offered her the job."

So that was that. She could sit across the table from him insisting she wanted a life back here but as soon as he pushed her toward her real world, she ran away without looking back.

Just like he knew she would. Why did he have to be so

damn right?

When he didn't say anything, Jake continued, "She told me to go ahead and lease the house to you and Lori. You'll have to give me a couple of weeks to get it cleaned up—"

"There's no rush. I'm not sure I can afford to do it anyway." Just days ago, getting him and his daughter into that house had been at the top of his goal list. Now, he couldn't imagine being within those walls without Hailey.

"But what about Lori and the horse she wanted?"

He backtracked. "You know what, a few weeks is good for me. I just need some time to put some things in order." *And my feelings.* Would weeks be enough time?

"Okay," Jake said, then turned for the door. After a few steps, he spun back. "Tell me it's none of my business, but I'm going to give you a little advice I've been carrying around for a while. Isolating Lori is just as bad for her as it is for you. You've both been hurt. For you, more than once by my sister, but locking both of you up away from people isn't a good defense from that pain. A life without risk, well, that's not really living. Is it?"

Nate took a couple of steps back and dropped down to his chair, resting his elbows on his knee and his forehead in his hands. "You don't have any idea."

"You're right. I don't know what you went through with your daughter's mom. I do know Hailey really cares about both of you. She didn't want to leave this time. Instead of giving in to her fears, she was willing to face them and give the two of you a chance."

Nate leaned over, pushing his fingers through his hair. "How can I keep her from everything she's ever wanted?"

"Why do you assume she doesn't want you?"

Jake didn't wait for Nate to respond, just turned and left the house, closing the door behind him.

Nate had reached for the brass ring once. He'd felt the cold metal against his fingertips, before it slipped from his grasp. And, here he landed.

Jake's point was valid. Moving through life day to day wasn't living. Neither was keeping Lori and him behind a wall.

And that's why he'd pushed Hailey away. Doing so now had to be better than watching her shrink away from everything she could be.

Nate forced himself out of his chair. The wait staff would be changing shifts at the diner and he called to let them know he wouldn't be back. The first "sick day" he'd taken in over a year.

Tomorrow was a new day, and he would step back into his old life.

Now, he was trying to construct a healthy, yet comforting dinner for his family, with the odds and ends he found in refrigerator. He'd decided on chicken and noodles and was chopping carrots when he heard Anna's car coming up the drive.

The clacking of the knife hitting the cutting board released the sadness that had morphed into something deeper.

When the back door opened, he turned to his sister and daughter with a painted on smile. "How was your day?"

Anna hung her coat up on the hook and then helped Lori. "Better than yours. Or so I'm hearing."

Lori struggled to begin speaking. "Why... fight with... Hailey?"

Nate tuned back to his food preparations, to avoid showing his daughter the depths of his pain. "News certainly travels fast."

Anna said, "We went by the restaurant. We wanted to surprise you and have dinner together."

"I had the same idea. Decided it was high time I made dinner for my own family instead of half the county."

He felt a tug on his pants and turned, looking down into the impatient eyes of his daughter. "I... like her."

Nate dropped down on one knee so he could look her in the eye, covering his mouth with his hand while he struggled to find the correct words. "I like her too, but she doesn't live around here. She belongs in New York."

"That's not what I heard." Anna sat down at the table. "Aunt Wanda says you pushed her away."

"She was going to pass up a fantastic job offer to stay here. That's not right. What was I supposed to say to her?"

"Stay." *You should have said "we want you to stay."* Lori signed then turned and ran from the room.

Nate stood and went back to cutting vegetables for a few seconds before tossing the knife back down to the counter. "Damn it! I should have listened to my gut and kept some distance between them."

"Don't blame Hailey for this, she didn't run. You pushed her away."

His sister was right, but he didn't want to admit it. Not now. He had a bigger issue to deal with than his own breaking heart and followed his daughter to her bedroom.

Through the cracked doorway he could see Lori sitting in the middle of her bed, picking at the knotted threads of the patchwork quilt. He knocked on the door and only entered when she looked up, making eye contact. He sat down on the side of the bed; picking up one of her plastic horses from the nightstand, he offered it to her.

She took it from him, laid it on her lap, and ran her fingers over the mane for a moment. *Why do people have to leave?*

"Honey, New York is where Hailey has lived for a long time. Her life is there. I told you that."

But Grandpa, Grandma, and my mom.

This wasn't the first time Lori had brought up the mother she'd never met, never known. It didn't hurt any less. "Grandma and Grandpa didn't leave you. They had to move to Arizona for Grandpa's health. They love us, and especially you, and are coming home this summer for a very long visit."

She nodded.

"I don't know what to say about your mother." Other than she was cold-hearted and he didn't have a clue what he'd seen in her in the first place. "But she's the one who's missing out, because you are a wonderful girl, who I love very, very, very much." He reached in and touched her chin, lifting it so he could look into her eyes.

"You said... you like... Hailey."

"I do. Very much."

"You should... have...t-t-told her."

"I can't." Weren't he and Lori the pair? It occurred to him the biggest reason he couldn't bring himself to ask her to stay was the very same fears that Lori had. He was sick and tired of people leaving too. And he couldn't bear to lose Hailey on any other terms than his own. He picked his daughter up and set her back down on his lap, hugging her tightly. "I promise you I'm never going to leave you. You know that, right?"

"Love you," she whispered in his ear. "You should... tell Hailey... we... want... her here."

****

Sure that Lori was screaming out in fitful sleep, Nate sat straight up in the bed. Instead, the house was silent. Eerily so. He reached out, grazing the pillow next to him. It still smelled vaguely like Hailey's perfume.

A searing pain ripped through his chest, as if his heart was being fed through a meat grinder. He picked up the pillow and brought it to him, resting his head on top of it.

His daughter's words echoed in his mind. *Tell Hailey.*

Just tell her. That he wanted her to stay. That he never stopped wanting her in his life. That the nights he'd spent with Lori's mother had been stupid, feeble attempts to get her out of his mind and heart.

Every woman he dated since was compared to Hailey.

What he felt for Hailey was more than a first crush. He couldn't let it slip through his fingers, not without really trying to make a go of it.

He picked up his smartphone from the nightstand, unplugged it from the charger, and brought up the web browser. After a few moments he was out of bed and into his jeans and a sweatshirt. He packed a duffle bag with a couple of changes of clothes. After tossing in the necessities from the bathroom, he made his way into Lori's room.

Turning on the light, he called. "Get up and get dressed, sweetie."

She sat up in the bed, rubbing the sleep from her eyes. "It's still... night."

"But we only have three and a half hours to make a plane, and it's a ninety minute drive."

"Where are we going?"

"To tell Hailey we want her to come home."

Chapter Twenty-Two

Hailey uncrossed and crossed her legs in the opposite direction, shifting her weight in the chair. The woman on the other side of the desk was her uncle's friend from college. The one who had offered her the job as a favor to him.

She had driven late into the night and returned to the road ridiculously early in order to make it home in time for the interview. Now, looking over the woman's shoulders and out the window to the Hudson River below made her homesick. In ways she couldn't explain—that didn't make any kind of sense—it reminded her of the beach. Her and Nate's beach.

Her first instinct when she opened her eyes at five o'clock this morning was to call him to say hello. He'd be on his way to open the diner and they could chat in the peaceful ease of the early morning.

Funny how something could become a habit in only a couple of days.

Then she remembered how they'd ended it.

She could feel the tears pushing against her eyes again and blinked hard, taking a deep breath before continuing. "I need to be assured that if a client comes to me with a case I feel passionate about, I have the discretion to take it."

"I hear what you're saying. Young idealism is something the partners really liked about you. However, this is a business. We have to stay in the black. I am sure that we can write your contract to include some leeway though. Maybe a certain number of cases a year we could trust to your discretion."

It was a more than fair offer—more than she could have hoped for given her age and work experience. She wasn't an A player, not at the top of her game. In fact, she was too young and too inexperienced to be making demands.

The fact that this woman was even considering her requests only confirmed that it was all part of Rhonda and her father's manipulations. Her family's attempts to keep her from throwing away a promising career.

No matter what Nate thought, the money didn't mean more to her than home, more than him.

Hailey looked down at her watch. Ninety seconds for her mind to swirl back to him. What was she doing here? No matter what her family wanted and what Nate thought, she knew she couldn't do this.

The walls were closing in, even the beautiful full glass one overlooking the water. Below was the city of concrete and steel that had once represented opportunity, choices, and the kind of life her little hometown could never give her. Now, it felt like a prison cell keeping her from the people she loved.

She stood. Picking up her purse and letting it hang off her shoulder, Hailey reached across the desk. "Thank you, ma'am, for the job offer. I can't tell you how much I appreciate your faith in me and your willingness to work with my goals, but I'm going to have to pass."

The woman took Hailey's hand. "I don't understand, your uncle said—"

"Yeah, my uncle doesn't understand either. They think they know what I want, but they are looking at an antiquated set of goals I set for myself a long time ago. If I've learned nothing else in the last year, it's what's important. I'm not going to let that slip through my fingers again."

"We're closed tomorrow for the holiday. Why don't you take a couple days to think about it?"

Holiday? That's right. It was New Year's Eve. Through everything that had happened the last few days, she'd lost track of the time, but the promise she'd made to Nate earlier in the week rang in her head. The only place she wanted to be at midnight was in his arms, kissing his lips, committing to a new, brighter future. "No. Thank you, but I don't need any more time to think about it. I've spent too much time thinking as it is. It's time to act."

The woman dropped back down behind her desk and shrugged. "I wish you the best, Miss Lambert. If you change your mind and want to get back in the big game, don't hesitate to call me."

With a certainty that trumped every feeling she'd had before this, Hailey left the office and fished her phone out of her purse. The only way she would be back in Nate's arms by midnight was to fly home.

But she didn't want to leave a single belonging here in the city. She knew that this life was her past. Her future— her home—was back in Caseville with Nate.

Whether or not he was ready to admit it was what he wanted too.

Unable to get a signal on the elevator, she waited until she was on the street to press on Nate's name on the screen. She held the phone to her ear and walked west toward the subway station.

It rang twice and then went to voice mail.

Damn him, anyway. Why did he have to be so stubborn? Why couldn't he accept that this was what she wanted?

She waited for the beep then said, "I'm coming home. You owe me a midnight kiss."

Dropping her phone into her purse as she rounded the corner to the steps of the subway station, she ran smack into someone.

Nate. But, it couldn't be.

It was.

His jaw dropped. "I can't believe, in this big, crazy, god-forsaken city—that I can't stand by the way—I would run right in to you."

"What are you doing here?"

He released Lori's hand and threw his arms around her. "I was so stupid. I can't live without you. And I came here to take you home."

A piece of her still remembered she was angry about how he'd pushed her away, but the bigger part of her that had just committed to making him take her back clung to him.

Nate squeezed her tighter and kissed her temple, before stepping back and gripping Lori's hand. No doubt the craziness of the traffic was overwhelming to her too. And it was much lighter than normal today given it was the holiday.

Hailey touched Nate's shoulder, leading them a dozen steps up the block. Standing in front of a restaurant, they were out of the flow of traffic. "How did you ever find me?"

"I called Rhonda, made her tell me your address and where your interview was. She didn't want to but eventually she gave in."

Hailey didn't know what to say. Nate had left his diner and got on a plane with his daughter, to brave the big unknown and find her.

"I know you've been offered everything you ever wanted here, and this," He looked around him motioning to the streets, "craziness is what you consider your home, but what Lori and I have—maybe that could be home. I don't know what the future holds, but I do know I don't want to give up on us so easily. You have to want it to, though. Don't come back with us unless you're sure you can be happy in our small town."

She could hear the tears cracking his voice and knew what it took for Nate to put his dented heart on the line. He was done teetering on the edge and willing to take that leap. As far as she was concerned, there was nothing left to consider. Hailey knew her heart, and Nate was finally ready to accept what he felt in his.

But then, there was one more person to consider.

Hailey turned her attention to Lori.

She hadn't said a word, only stood close to her father, observing everything said. Hailey dropped to one knee. "Is all of this okay with you? Do you mind if I move back home and date your father."

Lori's head quickly bobbed up and down. A wide smile turned her lips. "Yes. I want th-th-that."

Hailey stood and stepped closer to Nate, wrapping her arms around his waist. "I want to go home. Check your messages. I'd already decided. I turned down the job and called you to tell you I was coming to collect on my New Year's Eve kiss."

"Are you sure?"

"I'm positive. Can you stay here with me for a couple of days? I want to arrange to have all of my belongings shipped home and close out my lease. I don't want to leave anything behind. No more looking back. I only want to focus on the future."

He ran a finger through the piece of blonde hair framing her face. "I've always heard New Year in Time's Square is something everyone should experience."

She pulled her body tighter to his. "That's not what I had in mind."

****

Nate was amazed, and felt—finally—like he could see a happy future for him and his daughter. Just a week ago, he'd never guessed it would be in Hailey's company.

After connecting on the street, they went to the offices of a moving company where she'd scheduled a truck and arranged to have boxes delivered to her apartment, paying extra to have it done that afternoon.

He'd insisted they stop and have lunch, mostly because he and Lori hadn't eaten anything but a doughnut from the airport kiosk hours before.

She then brought them to her very small apartment in the West Village and began filling the boxes with her belongings. With he and Lori helping they'd made amazing progress in just a few hours.

Shortly after dinner, they'd filled the last of the boxes they had and would have to find a place to get a few more before the truck came the day after New Year. They would then drive her car back home.

Together.

Surprisingly, he'd found the ingredients to make a chocolate mousse dessert in her kitchen cupboards. Now, he dished his concoction into two bowls and put the remaining in the refrigerator, saving it for Lori who had fallen asleep on the floor waiting for midnight.

He then popped the cork on the bottle of champagne he'd bought at the corner store and filled glasses. In the living room, he set the dessert tray on the coffee table and rejoined Hailey under the blanket on her couch.

"And I thought my house was small." He pulled her closer, thrilling when she wrapped her arms around him and nuzzled into his chest.

"Space comes at a premium here. Besides, I've never needed more than this."

"Do you have any regrets?"

She shook her head slightly then sat up, reaching for a bowl of his dessert. "If I hadn't gone through college and law school here, I wouldn't have ever known what was really important. Besides, I still want to be a lawyer. I just want to do it back home, near you."

He picked up the other bowl, took a bite of the mousse than filled his spoon again offering it to her. "It's going to be difficult, building your practice from the ground up."

"I know. But I'm not worried. In case you haven't figured it out yet, I fight for what I want."

He kissed her lips lightly. "I've noticed."

The announcer on the TV began counting down the seconds to midnight. Hailey reached for the remote and turned it up a little. "Maybe I should have taken you down to Time's Square, after all. This could very well be your only chance to see it."

Nate laughed. As the camera scanned the crowd from overhead, he knew they'd made the right choice about the evening. As confetti began to fall and "Auld Lang Sine" began to play, Hailey moved in again. She wrapped her arms around his neck and made good on her vow to kiss him at midnight.

The first of many, he hoped.

In the soft glow from the lamp and television, they celebrated all the promises they'd made. There was no need to rehash it all with resolutions.

He was comfortable with all that was unspoken between them.

Hailey had kept her promise that they would celebrate this magical moment when one year rolled into the next with the traditional kiss. Nate had faith the second half of that promise—that it would be the first of many—would be fulfilled too.

THE END

Acknowledgements

Thank you to:

My husband, Brad Phillips, and my children, Joshua and Katelynn Phillips for always encouraging me to follow my dreams.

My dear friends who understand the ups and downs of this business and are always there with an ear when needed: Sloan Parker, Shay Lacy, Jenna Rutland, Jayne Kingston, Lesly Blanton, and Ray Wenck.

Kim Jacobs, Shelley Rawe for believing in this story as much as I did and helping to share it with the world.

S.R. Paulsen, my editor, for seeing the diamond in the rough, and giving me the guidance to bring it to the surface.

ABOUT CONSTANCE PHILLIPS

Constance Phillips lives in Ohio with her husband, daughter, and four canine kids. Her son, now on his own, is planning a wedding, reconfirming that romance still lives and breathes. When not writing stories of finding and rediscovering love, Constance and her husband spend the hours planning a cross-country motorcycle trip for the not-so-distant future…if they can find a sidecar big enough for the pups.

If you enjoyed Constance Phillips' *All That's Unspoken*, please consider telling others and writing a review.

An Excerpt From All That's Unclaimed
Book Two in The Sunnydale Days Series

Chapter One

To Ben Crawford the miles of fence surrounding the seventy-five acres of Sunnydale Farms did not just contain his mother's horses. Those rails also held him back from some abstract calling he hadn't yet heard.

This therapeutic riding stable was Betty Crawford's dream, born out of her desire to help a friend's daughter. The undeniable benefits of equine therapy on that autistic child sparked a fire in his mother. She did her research, trained with the North American Riding for the Handicapped Association, and began switching the focus of her stables from a 4H barn to a facility that helped the physically and emotionally challenged.

Sunnydale Farms was born, at least in concept.

Ben found satisfaction as well. Helping people heal challenged him, and working alongside his mother allowed him to combine his love of horses and youngsters. But something was missing.

Walking the long corridor between the two rows of stalls, the heel of Ben's boot clacked against the concrete only a little louder than the sound of horses munching on their grain. The familiar sounds mingling with the smell of lilacs blooming reminded him he was home again.

Instead of taking comfort, he felt constrained, as if he was stuck in a pair of riding boots that were a size too small.

He pulled the clipboard from the nail on the bulletin board and looked at the schedule of riding students. They were double-booked all day, a sure sign of summer vacation. He only had one break: thirty minutes around one o'clock.

The upside: he got to share the arena with Anna Jenkins.

She'd been hired as a teen—the summer before he left for college—to fill the void created by his absence. A high school junior at the time, Anna happily plowed through even the messiest of chores without complaint. Her work ethic was fueled by the desire to be surrounded by horses. He never understood her particular enthusiasm for forking through wood shavings, but he welcomed a break from mucking stalls and never questioned it.

Later, she proved her dedication to both the Crawfords and the children by obtaining her training certification from the NARHA.

Over recent years, he'd come home at intervals, only to leave after a few months for more schooling or job opportunities. Somehow, something always drew him back.

Last winter, it'd been a wedding. Anna served as a bridesmaid at her brother's nuptials. It was the first and only time he'd seen her in a dress or her long, brown hair styled in a way other than neatly pulled off her face by a gray knit headband. In an instant, she went from schoolgirl barn help to a full-grown woman.

Now, every time she showed kindness to a child or paid focused attention to the animals, the act would bathe her in an angelic glow. He also noticed the jeans and ragged T-shirts accented her slight waist and full hips better than the bridesmaid's gown that first grabbed his libido.

The sound of Anna humming as she entered the barn turned him in her direction. She paused in front of the stall that housed the new mare before continuing down the aisle and stopping in front of him. She wiped her hands on the small towel she'd connected to a belt loop of her jeans with a metal clip. "Do you think it's a good idea for your mom to start training that mare already?"

"You know what Mom is like. She was up half the night outlining a schedule."

"It might be wiser to let the horse settle in a bit, get used to the surroundings."

"Mom won't get on her today. Just groom her, maybe do a little ground work."

"But inside the stall?" Anna shifted her weight and turned her gaze back toward the end of the aisle. The look in her eyes confused Ben.

The new horse was a five-year-old and completely green, but his mother could handle anything life threw at her, always had for as long as he could remember.

He tapped the clipboard in his hands. "Are you with me? We need to go over today's schedule."

She nodded, but he could tell she only half listened to him. "What time did your mom get back with the horse last night?"

"After eleven."

"How did she come off the trailer?"

He unsuccessfully tried to contain the laugh. "Fine! My mother has been around horses since she was younger than your niece. She can handle a spirited mare."

Rotating her shoulders as if she could shake off the bad feelings, she turned back toward him. "I know. I..."

She paused and adjusted that trademark headband. "It's just that from the first time we looked at that horse, she spooked me. There's something about it that I just don't like."

Hearing that admission set off an alarm in Ben's gut. On his list of fearless women—right under Betty Crawford—was Anna's name. Her ability to handle chaos was only one of the many attributes he admired about her. When one of their young students melted down or a horse behaved badly, she took charge and diffused the situation with sympathy or sternness, whichever the situation called for. She had an uncanny ability to catch any monkey wrench thrown into the events of the day, circumventing any potential crisis. "Nothing frightens you."

She laughed. "I wish."

"Seriously. Name one thing you're afraid of."

"Running out of chocolate."

She maintained such a serious look on her face while making the joke. Yet another endearing quality he'd come to adore in her. Her laugh erupted again, which penetrated his emotional walls, crumbling the business atmosphere he struggled to maintain.

He reached out and tugged on the sleeve of her T-shirt. "Come on. We need to figure out which students should ride what horses. I think I should use Honey with John. Do you want to use Ginger with Cory?"

A piercing bray rose up from the end of the aisle.

"Whoa! Whoa!" His mother's shrill cry cut the air.

Two loud bangs against the stall wall.

Then silence.

"You okay, Betty?" Fear rode Anna's question, intensifying the tremble whisking up Ben's spine.

No screams. No sound at all.

Anna sprinted down the aisle. The clipboard slipped from Ben's hand, rattling against the concrete. He followed behind her, calling out his mother's name and hoping for an answer.

Any answer.

Anna reached the stall first. "Dear God."

The horror in her eyes hedged him. Ben knew he didn't want to see what she did, but he couldn't let fear corral him and looked around the corner.

Betty Crawford lay in a crumpled heap in the far corner. Lifeless. The horse had pushed itself into the opposite corner and now looked calm.

Anna grabbed the lead rope that hung on a nail and reached for the stall door handle.

Ben quickly covered her hand with his much larger one. His mom had drilled protocol on how to handle this kind of emergency into his head. He instinctively fell into crisis mode.

Anna argued against his restraint. "She's not moving!"

"I know. After I get the horse out of the stall, you stay with her while I call 911." If he could hear the tremor in his

155

voice, the horse would sense his distress. This was a time for calm heads. He needed to be firm and in control so the animal would not spook or rear up.

Swallowing hard, he took the lead rope from Anna and guided her to the side, before taking sure, purposeful steps, keeping his eyes focused on the young mare. He grabbed the halter and hooked the clip to the ring.

"Be careful," Anna said.

With a single tug, the horse followed Ben out of the stall.

After turning her loose in the arena and securing the gate, Ben dialed 911 on his cell phone then ran the length of barn. When the dispatcher answered, he requested an ambulance and gave the woman their address.

Ben knelt in the stall's bedding next to Anna. "How is she? Is she breathing?"

"Yes. Still unconscious. And all this blood! She must have hit her head. And look at her shoulder. I don't want to move her."

"No. Don't." Into the phone he repeated the list of obvious injuries Anna had just enumerated.

He watched as Anna smoothed his mother's hair off her face and patted her hand. Speaking quietly, she reassured the woman they were both there and the ambulance was on the way.

For some odd reason, Ben remembered Anna at her brother's wedding. That night he'd seen her outer beauty in clear focus. In this moment, he realized her character matched the glamorous image.

He could hear sirens in the distance, maybe a mile away. "They're almost here, Mom. We'll get you to the hospital soon."

Anna pushed herself to her feet. "I'll go open the gates."

She maneuvered her way out of the stall, and from the sound of her footfalls, he could tell she ran at top speed.

Thank God she's here.

He moved closer to his mom and squeezed her hand

tight as Anna had done. The dispatcher rambled in his ear, asking again for the details of the accident.

"I told you I didn't see what happened!"

Maybe he should have. He couldn't remember the last time he'd seen his mom so excited about a horse. Still, excitement never clouded her judgment before. Anna knew the horse was dangerous and had told his mom so. The two usually relied on each other's judgment, but this mare had stolen his mother's heart.

Why hadn't Anna come to him about this earlier? He was supposed to be his mother's right hand on the farm, yet the two women always kept him in the dark.

They adjusted horse's feed, scheduled rider's appointments, and placed orders, never asking for Ben's input. Every time he returned from months in Seattle or Miami or Biloxi, with new certifications and fresh insights from the wonderful work done in hospitals and other training barns, he would unpack his bags and prepare to lay out his new ideas for Anna and his mother. They always seemed pleased to have him back, but he never got the feeling they wanted anything but man hours from him. He knew they'd developed their system while he was gone but couldn't help wondering if maybe he'd stayed away too long overall to ever be considered an important part of the facility's operations.

The sirens grew louder as the ambulance approached the barn. Obviously anxious, the horses in the surrounding stalls began to whinny and pace.

Ben fumbled to shove the phone into his back pocket after the dispatcher hung up. "Over here! Last stall on the right!"

At the sound of a gurney rolling down the aisle, he found his feet and backed out of the stall just as the two paramedics pushed their way in. One was holding a large black box. The other held a neck brace.

Ben struggled to follow the conversation between the paramedics, even though he knew some medical terminology. Being a licensed physical and occupational therapist wasn't the same as being a doctor, and the speed at which they spoke, mixed with his fear for his mother, made it hard for him to completely process their main concerns.

Anna stopped in front of him, barely winded even thought she had run for all she was worth. She rubbed his arm. "Don't worry about anything but your mother. I'll take care of the horses and everything here."

Panic rose up. "What? No! Cancel all the lessons for today and come to the hospital. I don't want to wait alone."

She eyed him curiously. "Are you sure that's what you want me to do?"

"Yes. I'll go with the ambulance. Come as quick as you can secure everything."

"Of course."

"Thanks." His words rode a tremble and his legs went light as the severity of his mother's injuries began to come into focus. Ben twisted away from Anna, peeking into the stall. His mother still lay motionless as the paramedics continued their treatment, securing his mother to a backboard and locking the neck brace into place. He leaned back against the stall. He couldn't lose the only parent who'd ever been there for him.

He'd been eight when his father had abandoned both of them to chase the dream of rodeo stardom. After ten semi-successful years, Sam Crawford returned to the area hoping to rebuild the lost relationships. Ben left for college a few months after Sam's return and avoided dealing with his deadbeat dad. Betty, on the other hand, agreed to let the past go and remained friendly with her ex. For Ben, it would always be too little, way too late.

The image of the blood soaking her hair and her disjointed shoulder and arm flashed through his mind. His hands curled into fists.

She'd come through this. He'd accept no less

His body sank further down the wall, and he pushed his weight against it, trying to stay upright. Anna stepped closer. Her hands braced his shoulders. "Your mother is the strongest, bravest woman I know. She's going to be okay."

Ben's arms ached with a need to be wrapped around Anna. He should tell her all the crazy mixed-up feelings that had been recently swirling in his head. Why couldn't he say he wanted to lean against her for support instead of the barn wall?

This was a work place. And she was an employee. So, he reached out and patted her shoulder.

The paramedics wheeled his mother out of the stall and down the aisle.

A fog swirled around him and his feet felt light as they carried him to the ambulance. He followed the paramedics' directions, pulling himself up into the back and taking a seat on the small rail attached to the metal wall.

Wake up!

This was just a horrible nightmare.

Right?

It had to be.

In the ambulance, the paramedic worked on his mother. Ben refused to let go of her hand, even if she wasn't conscious. Even if she didn't know he was there.

He tried to focus on the questions asked.

Did the horse hit her in the head?

Was the injury from being slammed into the stall wall?

What about her shoulder?

Repeatedly, he told them he hadn't witnessed the accident, only heard his mother's scream and then the loud noises. His best guess: the horse kicked her into the stall wall.

Twice.

The paramedic's questions and continual examination of her neck caused Ben to wonder if she had a spinal injury to go with the obvious broken bones.

The sirens cut through his ability to concentrate. Their continual wail signaled the severity of her injuries. This wasn't a big city. Sirens weren't a necessity to clear traffic.

Usually, an ambulance would just blast them on at intersections.

They were getting closer, had to be. The barn was only six miles from the hospital, and the driver raced down the country roads as if they were a NASCAR track.

His mother tightened her grip on his hand at the same time her moan hit his ear.

"Mom! Can you hear me?"

"Benny." She struggled, her words soft. Her eyes remained closed.

"I'm right here. We'll be at the hospital soon."

"Call your dad."

Why is that rat-bastard the first person to jump to her mind?
"What?"

"Your dad." She paused, squeezed again. "He can help Anna around the barn."

"I can help Anna!"

"And train Philomena."

Philo-who? Of course. The mare.

Made in the USA
Monee, IL
10 April 2021

65220695R00095